Summer Loving

20 Sultry Stories

Edited by Alison Tyler
Foreword by Angell Brooks

eXcessica publishing

Summer Loving © 2014

All rights reserved under the International and Pan-American Copyright Conventions. No part of this book may be reproduced or transmitted in any form or by any means, electronic or mechanical, including photocopying, recording, or by any information storage and retrieval system, without permission in writing from the publisher.

This is a work of fiction. Names, places, characters and incidents are either the product of the author's imagination or are used fictitiously, and any resemblance to any actual persons, living or dead, organizations, events or locales is entirely coincidental. All sexually active characters in this work are 18 years of age or older.

This book is for sale to ADULT AUDIENCES ONLY. It contains substantial sexually explicit scenes and graphic languge which may be considered offensive by some readers. Please store your files where they cannot be access by minors.

Excessica LLC
P.O. Box 127
Alpena MI 49707

To order additional copies of this book, contact:
books@excessicapublishing.com
www.excessica.com

Cover art © 2014 Willsin Rowe

Warning: the unauthorized reproduction or distribution of this copyrighted work is illegal. Criminal copyright infringement, including infringement without monetary gain, is investigated by the FBI and is punishable by up to 5 years in prison and a fine of $250,000.

Table of Contents

Foreword	7
Introduction	11
Moon Lovers	13
Housework Can Wait	19
Heat upon Heat	23
Fireworks Display	29
Summer Surrender	33
Tell Me	39
Summer Lightning	45
To Hell with Sunset	51
The Chaperone	55
Hot as Ice	61
Protection	65
An Oven on Broil	69
Summer in December	75
Splash	83
Hot Tomato	87
Arizona, Ireland, New England	93
Baby, It's Hot Outside	99
Summer School	105
Night Swimming	111
When in Nice	117
About the Authors	121

Foreword

Hot Fun in the Summertime. Boys of Summer. Summer in the City.

Musicians love the heat wave that hits us in the middle of the year. The weather gets almost unbearably hot, with people sweating and sticking to each other, sweltering and melting. There's swimming, and outdoor play, and lots, and LOTS, of skin. And to cool off? Well, choose any number of cold treats, from ice cream to frozen margaritas.

Summer is a wonderful season.

And the twenty writers who penned some fabulous heat-inducing tales all agree.

Sommer is definitely our favorite season. And no, that's not a typo.

The Internet is an amazing thing. It can band strangers together through a common interest faster than any medium that has ever existed. You can communicate, and become best friends with, people you might never meet in real life. But through the magic of modern communication, you can be with them through their most accomplished feats, and through their most terrifying moments.

I first "met" Sommer Marsden about six years ago, through a comment she made on Alison Tyler's blog. I started following the pithy, creative, sensually amusing genius. We started communicating. I started to adore her. I've read just about everything she's ever written, and loved it all. She's inspired me in my writing, and been there to give advice, support, and a kick in the ass when it's needed most.

Many of us in the erotica community feel that way about each other. Most have never met—but some are lucky enough to venture away from our keyboards and see the faces and hear the voices behind the screen names. But even if we don't, that doesn't stop the love.

When Sommer came to us with the news that her husband—known to us in the community as "the man"—had cancer, we were stunned. It's a horrible thing and has affected almost every one of us in some way.

It was the incredible Alison Tyler who sent out the call for this collection: Subs for Sommer, about summer. Sexy, sweet, short stories to go in an anthology to help one of the most generous and amazing writers we are all fortunate to know—to help her and her family in one of the most trying times of their lives. The stories poured in, and Alison has been going cross-eyed putting this book together.

I've never spoken to Sommer, not on the phone or in person. But I don't have to see her to know that she's strong, capable, talented, entertaining, and ... well, the list could go on forever. We're writers after all. We're good with our words.

In this book, you'll find that the authors are more than good with words—they're exceptional. No matter what the weather is outside, I can guarantee you'll be stripping down to nothing while enjoying baking on the beach, or picnics in the park.

Or sex in the swimming pool.

We're coming together for Sommer.

Save me a sno-cone.

—Angell Brooks

Introduction

This project has rendered me speechless. And as I am a girl who loves her words, that doesn't happen to me very often. Sommer Marsden is my best friend I've never met. We connected on New Year's Day 2007—and we have been as inseparable as two people can be who live on opposite coasts. To sum up Sommer in a nutshell is to say this: If I were working on a charity project for another author, Sommer would be the first writer to come to me with a story, and it would be hot.

She is giving. She is kind. She is quick-witted. And she is funny as fuck.

This book was the brainchild of Tamsin Flowers. Hundreds of writers submitted stories. I had originally thought that I'd use all of them—until I saw how many there were! With behind-the-scenes help, I ended up choosing twenty. The stories are sweet, scorching, sublime, satisfying and supremely selected for Sommer.

Selena Kitt at eXcessica graciously offered to publish the book and give the proceeds to Sommer. Willsin Rowe delivered the divine cover. Angell Brooks penned a foreword that brought tears to my eyes. Sophia Valenti proofed every word.

When cancer hit my life five years ago, Sommer was there when I had my nineteenth nervous breakdown. She virtually held my hand. She never left. I know we can't do everything I'd like to be able to do for her. But we did this, and we all hope this helps—more than words can say.

XXX,
Alison Tyler

Moon Lovers
By Donna George Storey

I asked Melissa if she wanted go to the beach on Saturday to catch some summer sun and salt air.

She smiled and shook her head. "I burn like a lobster unless I'm double-dipped in SPF 75. But fortunately it happens to be the perfect weekend for moonbathing."

And so I found myself on her doorstep at eleven that Saturday night, dressed in my swim trunks. She said she'd provide the "moonscreen" and towels. Melissa had some crazy ideas, but I'd learned to go with the flow. Sex with her was out of this world.

She greeted me in a beach robe, her pretty feet bare. Taking my hand, she led me to her back porch. I stood there in silence, taking it all in. The terrace was transformed into some kind of roofless bedroom. A sheet-covered air mattress floated in the center of the deck. Citronella candles circled it like an altar. The railings were draped with beach towels—I noticed one had a cartoon sun wearing sunglasses—effectively shielding our activities from the neighbors' view. The value-pack of condoms I kept at her place was beside the bed. And above us, a fat July moon spilled cool shadows over the fuck nest below.

My cock stirred.

She stretched out on the mattress and beckoned me to join her. When she pulled her robe open, she was totally nude underneath. And I was at full mast.

I laughed and asked her if she was cold.

"A little, but I don't like to get moonlines. Could you put some of this on my back for me?" She handed me a tube of body lotion and rolled over on her stomach.

I was more than happy to rub the gooey, white stuff all over her back and ass and thighs. She made soft noises of pleasure as I massaged her, but she wouldn't turn over and let things follow their natural course. She wanted to give her back a full twenty minutes of moon exposure, she explained. She even set a timer.

So I asked her to tell me more about moonbathing. Did she lie on her porch naked in the moonlight every night?

My question amused her. "The moon has to be almost full, so there are really only about four nights a month you get the total effect—and I can't do it in the winter. Catching a cold would outweigh the benefits."

Which were?

"Moonbeams give fair complexions a special glow."

True enough, Melissa did have unusually luminous skin.

She gave me a sly smile. "Plus moonbeams affect my libido in a... positive way, but I probably shouldn't have told you about that."

Of course, I pressed her for the details. Finally, she confessed, although I'm sure that's what she wanted all along. "It's strange, but even when it's chilly, under the moonlight my body starts to get warm all over. It feels so good I just can't resist, you know, touching myself."

The image of Melissa masturbating on her deck by the light of the full moon got me all roused up again. But wasn't she afraid someone would see her?

"Of course, he sees me. That's what makes it so hot."

He?

"The man in the moon. He's lonely up there in his silver kingdom."

Just then the timer went off in a trill of beeps.

Melissa dutifully rolled onto her back. But unlike a sunbather, she bent her knees and tilted her hips up, giving that glowing voyeur's eye up in the sky a pretty good view of the treasures between her soft thighs. Oddly enough, I was starting to feel jealous.

I asked her how he would feel about watching me touch her.

She glanced at me and looked away. Even in the darkness, I could tell she was blushing. "Actually, I think he'd like that. He likes to watch my pleasure."

Did he indeed? Well, why not give the guy a show? I brushed her nipple with my fingertips. She sighed and her legs fell open a little more. I rested my other hand over her mons. She was already very, very wet and swollen. I flicked her clit lazily. She moaned, but she didn't turn her head into the pillow the way she usually did. Instead, she gazed straight up at the moon, a faint smile playing over her lips.

I doubled my efforts—for his benefit or hers, I wasn't sure—rubbing her between her legs and suckling her beautiful breasts until she was squirming and hot all over.

I asked her if he could see how wet she was, juicing up the sheet with her desire.

"Yes, god, yes," she hissed. "Now take off your bathing suit. He wants to see your big, hard cock, too."

She was really far gone in this moon fantasy, but her strange request brought me closer to my goal—which was to bury said big, hard cock inside her. I slithered out of my trunks and reached for a condom, but she put a trembling hand on my arm.

"Lie back and let him look at you, too. You won't be sorry."

She ran her warm hand over my belly and thighs to reassure me. What did I really have to lose if I went along with her lunacy?

Yet, as I lay there exposing myself to the summer sky, my hard-on was suddenly bathed in the weirdest sensation—a tingling, both cool and warm. My dick felt harder than a bar of steel, ready to go at it all night long.

"He wants to watch me fuck you." I wasn't quite sure where those words came from, but it was my lips speaking them.

"Yes, I know," she said. "Let him watch us do it."

Condoms usually blunt the sensation, but my moon-drenched cock was still buzzing as I pushed into her slick cunt. We moved together, both desperate with need. As I thrust in and out, my buttocks started throbbing with that same cool-hot fire, licking into my cleft like a greedy tongue. I bucked hard and burrowed deeper than I'd ever gone before. She clutched me and cried out. Her pussy flooded with that extra juice that always means she's climaxed.

Then it got really crazy. My ass burned hotter, as if I'd been spanked—or out in the sun too long. All the while that phantom silver tongue worked my asshole, a dizzying, celestial rim job, as if in reward for showing that poor bastard in the moon what he could never have.

In the next instant, I shot like a geyser, opalescent fireworks exploding against my eyelids.

"Now wasn't that more fun than sand in your shoes and a sunburn?" she whispered as we lay together under the star-flecked sky.

I stared up at the moon, who looked rather satisfied in his perch above us. I still wasn't quite sure what had just happened, but with Melissa, I'd learned to go with the flow.

Once again, the sex was out of this world.

Housework Can Wait
By Sophia Valenti

The first slap always stings the most, and I reared up, gasping as Cameron's hand connected sharply with my bare ass. Not missing a beat, he nudged my head downward to put me back in my place, which was over his lap. I tried to mentally prepare myself for the onslaught, but I knew that was impossible. Cam rested his palm on the small of my back—a silent command for me to hold still—while his other hand rained down a series of steady blows that left me whimpering. But I knew that was only the beginning. The sharp bursts of pain he continued to deliver faded into a deep, pulsing heat that made my pussy thump in time with its sinful rhythm.

Not thirty minutes earlier I'd come in from work, sticky and cranky from my trip home in a train without air-conditioning. My hair was plastered to my neck and face, and I quickly scooped up the wayward strands into a ponytail as I kicked off my high heels.

"Another fare hike, and this is what we get," I muttered, peeling off my dress. The formfitting sheath had looked classy and crisp during my morning meeting, but it was now a damp, wrinkled mess. I tossed the garment onto the couch, right next to Cameron. He looked at it, and then back at me, without saying a word. I padded over and took his lemonade out of his hand. After taking a sip, I put the glass on the table and proceeded to wiggle out of my pantyhose and leave them on the floor. As I uselessly fanned myself with my hand, he arched an eyebrow at my histrionics.

Since I'd left the sweltering train, the heat wasn't all that bad. I just needed a few moments to cool down, but when I became aware of the way Cameron was staring at me—with that wicked gleam in his sky-blue eyes—my temperature continued to rise.

"So, uh, what'd you do with your day off?" My question was a foolish attempt at casual conversation, as if I could make him forget the devious plan that seemed to be churning in his head. I couldn't, of course, but I liked to pretend. It's always the same: I hope those extra seconds I'm buying myself will allow me to stir up some sort of courage, but that never comes to pass.

"What'd I do?" he responded, glancing at my rumpled dress and discarded shoes and hose. "I'd straightened out the living room," he deadpanned.

"Oh!" I felt my face flush as my gaze followed his, taking in my path of destruction. In the back of my mind, I remembered thinking that the room had looked more tidy—that is, before I'd decorated it with my dirty laundry.

"I can tell you had a rough trip home," Cameron lectured, "but that's no excuse for undoing all of my hard work." My man's voice had dropped into that husky zone that makes my nipples spike, and I could feel them doing just that inside my sheer pink bra.

I swallowed hard, trying to think of a response that would get me off the hook. But we'd played this game enough for me to know that nothing would save me.

"I'm sorry, Cameron," I whispered, my nervousness making my voice crack. "I'll clean it up." I'd bent to fetch my dress, when Cameron grabbed me around the waist and dumped me over his lap.

"You will," he assured me, yanking down my panties, "but only after you've been punished."

I felt a twinge in my clit upon hearing that last word: punished. I feared it as much as I craved it. But all of my thoughts evaporated instantly as the first spank landed. My face heated with embarrassment as Cameron continued to chastise me for being so messy and not appreciating all that he did around the house.

Another apology was swirling in my head, but my mouth couldn't create the words. Instead, my whimpers and moans joined the noise of his hand clapping against my rear in an all too familiar soundtrack. As I writhed in his lap, I could feel Cameron's erection swelling beneath me. I always think I'll be able to stay still and stoically take my punishment, but that's never the case. My antics make Cameron spank me even harder, but from the way he pushes his hips up toward me in time with his relentless hand, he enjoys my petulance more than he'd ever admit.

As much as my ass ached and burned, I could also feel that my thighs had grown slick with my arousal. It was a detail that hadn't escaped my boyfriend.

"Spread for me, baby," he ordered gruffly. Knowing what was coming next, I parted my thighs with no small amount of hesitation.

I held my breath and then released it in a rush as he slapped my wet slit. His fingertips hit my clit so sharply, the contact felt like an electric shock. I moaned loudly as Cameron upped the tempo, repeatedly spanking my pussy until my climax burst suddenly and intensely, leaving me limp.

Cam nudged me off his lap, and I knelt on the floor between his thighs as he freed his erection from his pants. Without waiting for instruction, I swooped down and took him in deep. He held my head firmly, thrusting his hips upward and fucking my face until he shot his cream across my tongue. I swallow as much of each burst as I could, and when he'd shivered through his last spasm, he released me and I sat back on my heels.

Cameron leaned down to kiss me. "Housework can wait," he murmured against my lips. "Let's see how messy we can make the bedroom."

Heat upon Heat
By Lucy Felthouse

Cecily couldn't tear herself away from the window. Not that she'd tried very hard. She should have been out there, under the sky, under the burning sun. Instead, she stood in the shadows of her bedroom, hoping like hell he didn't look up and see her standing there, watching him.

He was Ashley, the young man her aunt had hired to replace and paint her garden fence. He was only a few months older than Cecily, almost twenty-two, and he had a body to die for and was currently showing it off as he worked, topless.

She stared, utterly entranced, as he bent and lifted and stretched and painted. His muscles flexing and releasing, his body lithe, tight, strong. The sun beamed down on him, bathing him in light, highlighting the sheen of sweat that covered his beautiful body.

Cecily wanted to lick it off him. Lick every droplet of sweat like he was the world's tastiest ice cream. Maybe she'd then cover him in actual ice cream and lick that off, too.

He looked like a Greek god, and she wanted to worship him. Pull those low-slung shorts down, then his underwear—if he wore any—and take his cock into her mouth, taste the perspiration and the sunshine. Suck and slurp at his shaft until he came in her mouth, filling her until she overflowed, dribbling his nectar down her chin and onto her chest.

It wasn't just his body that was delicious, though. His face was also perfection—brown hair that had that just-fucked look. Blue eyes that resembled the deepest ocean. Lips so sinful they should come with a warning. A jaw that appeared chiseled from the finest granite.

Cecily watched as Ashley made light work of the awkward fence panels. Her aunt was out, and therefore not supervising him, but he still worked as hard as he had been when Aunt Teresa was there. So he was good-looking, hardworking and honest. Was there no end to the man's perfection?

He paused, swiped the back of his hand across his forehead, removing the moisture that had gathered there.

Suddenly, Cecily imagined him naked in a cold shower. The chilly water sluicing all the stickiness away, cleaning him. So then she could make him all dirty again. Sweaty, panting. Rolling around in a tangle of crisp sheets, limbs linking, hair standing on end, rocking together.

He was so perfect, so godlike, that he had to be a spectacular fuck, too. His long thick cock would part her pussy lips, stretch her wide, ride her to a blissful climax. She'd hold on to his firm arse cheeks as he did, wrap her legs around his, jerk her hips, pull him deeper, harder.

She couldn't help it; she pushed her hand down under the waistband of her shorts, into her knickers, touched herself. She found her cunt already wet and ready, swollen and slick with thoughts of the handsome man in the garden. Thoughts of him fucking her, thoughts of her fucking him.

She closed her eyes, let the sexy mental images take over, fill her mind, fill the blank canvas behind her eyelids. The fantasies became more graphic, more heated, and she moved her hand faster, stroked her distended clit harder, wishing she had something long and thick to stuff in her cunt as she masturbated to dirty imaginings of Ashley.

Her chest heaved, her breaths grew rapid as she teased her body closer and closer to orgasm, her imagination firing her up as much as her touch, if not more.

She was nearly there—her body grew tight, a tingle began in her groin, radiated out. Just a few more strokes...

"Cecily?" A deep, sexy voice broke her reverie, her concentration. Her climax sunk like an anchor, into the depths of her disappointment. Stunned, she turned around, only snatching her hand from her knickers when it was too late. He'd already seen. Seen that she was wanking. At least he didn't know what about. Though her position at the window probably gave him a damn good idea. Fuck.

His gorgeous eyes darkened as he continued to look at her. A smile curved his sinful lips. "I just came to tell you I'm finished for the day." He stepped towards her. "But now I can see I'm not. Not by a long shot."

Cecily soon realized he was nothing like her fantasies. He was a million times better. He grabbed her and pushed her onto the bed, quickly covering her body with his. The heat from his sun-baked skin seeped through her thin vest-top and mingled with her own warmth. Heat upon heat, it threatened to melt her, to make her spontaneously combust.

And that was before he even kissed her. Once he captured her lips with his, slipped his tongue into her mouth and rocked his hips gently against hers, she was lost. The dampness in her knickers increased tenfold and she wanted nothing more than for her fantasies to come true. Right away.

She couldn't speak, couldn't voice her need as Ashley wouldn't stop kissing her. And when he eventually did, the things he did to her were so utterly decadent that he rendered her silent. His lips trailed down her chin, her neck, her chest. He tugged off her top, her bra and sucked and licked her until she was a writhing mass of need.

The shorts went, along with the sodden knickers. Ashley pressed his mouth to her cunt, and within seconds he'd brought her back to the edge of the orgasm she'd lost when he walked in on her. She had no time to worry about her own sweat as his talented lips and tongue gave her what she so desperately wanted; a climax that far surpassed any she'd ever had by her own hand or by that of someone else.

Her Greek god had otherworldly skills, and he spent the rest of the long, hot summer demonstrating them on her eager body. Demonstrations she happily returned.

Fireworks Display
By Emerald

I had decided to forego the usual Fourth of July parties and gatherings and watch the fireworks by myself this year. About a half hour before dark, I drove to the nearby college where the municipal fireworks were to be launched from the football field, found a parking spot, and sat back to wait, planning to watch the show from my car.

Cars continued to stream into the lot around me as the sun set. Most people got out and headed for seats on the bleachers or carried blankets to find a spot on the ground. As I opened the sunroof, a silver king cab pickup pulled up and parked in the row behind me, one spot to the left. The raucous laughter of the occupants was audible before they even got out, and I glanced in my side mirror.

All four doors of the vehicle opened, and I watched as one young male figure after another emerged. All in all the truck was full of six young men, probably in their early twenties. I ogled them shamelessly in the mirror, knowing they didn't see me and likely didn't even realize anyone was in the car. They all climbed on top of the cover over the truck bed, conversing noisily.

A low heat started in my stomach. Cock times six was arranged just a few feet behind me, and they didn't even know I was there. I dropped my hand to my lap. Deftly, I undid my jeans and wiggled my fingers into my panties. My eyes stayed on the mirror as I massaged my clit as much as I could with my jeans on, imagining myself on my knees in front of the six boys. I pictured them all lined up in a row, each shooting his load all over my face until I was coming, breathing heavily as the loud voices continued obliviously behind me.

A searing whistle broke the night seconds later, followed by a large boom as a huge white firework burst like popcorn in the air. Its earsplitting crackle bounced off the horizon as each spark dispersed into a tiny smattering of fuchsia lights.

I shifted and refastened my jeans, then scooted over and rose up through the open sunroof, facing the field as I leaned on the roof of my car. The conversation behind me paused, and I knew I had caught the attention of the assemblage. I could almost feel their eyes on the bare skin of my back below the ties of my flag-patterned halter.

The dull orange glow of the parking lot lights made all six of them just visible as I glanced over my shoulder and saw them all looking at me. I smiled casually and turned back to the pyrotechnic display in front of us. Knowing I was under the watchful eye of six boys likely ten years my junior made my breath shudder slightly as I drew it in. I reached back to tighten the tie on my top, desperately tempted to pull the strings and let it fall, to let the six behind me see the tie slip from my neck and know I was topless in front of them with my tits exposed to the night—even though all they could see was my naked back.

But I tightened the strings as planned and lowered my hands. They shook a bit.

I shifted to stand on the center console and hoisted myself onto the roof of my car. My legs dangled through the sunroof as I leaned back on my elbows, the tops of my breasts possibly visible now to the audience behind me. A cluster of about half a dozen fireworks went up simultaneously, the distant crowd *oohing* and *aahing* at the influx of echoing cracks. The largest was an eye-catching violet, its disc of sparks hovering in front of the others as the pyrotechnic perimeter spread.

I glanced over my shoulder again. Six pairs of eyes immediately found mine. Even if we had wanted to talk to each other, the noise of the fireworks display would have smothered any opportunity. They were relegated by necessity to pure voyeurs, with me—the exhibitionist—a lone figure competing against a backdrop of spectacular light and fire.

The thunderous noise paused. The sky was ebony, wisps of stray gray smoke lingering like breath bated in anticipation of the finale, which all watching knew was coming.

Like a pyrotechnic orgasm, multiple lights shot instantaneously into the air and blew up, fiery hues exploding into formations overlapping, embracing and kissing, like an orgy of sparks coming again and again. Purple, white, green, red, sparkling, glowing, spiraling as I forgot momentarily about the audience behind me and let the eruption hold my breath in its fleeting climax.

The distant audience clapped. My breath was quick, the adrenaline called up by the resplendent display already starting to dissipate like the smoke covering the sky. Without turning around, I reached up and yanked the string on my top. The fabric dropped forward, leaving nothing between the charged night air and my breasts. I placed my hands over them and turned, twisting my body toward the six young men. Each one's gaze was already zeroed in on me.

With a breathless giggle, I pulled my hands away.

Six mouths dropped open in unison. I gave a little grin and dropped through the sunroof into the driver's seat, retying my top and then starting the car. Shifting quickly, I pulled forward just ahead of the throng of departing spectators as they engulfed the parking lot behind me. I beamed as I zipped to the exit and turned onto the highway, the receding campus fading from view before the smoke above it had even cleared.

Summer Surrender
By Jodie Griffin

Silence.

It was far quieter than she'd expected. She couldn't hear anything but the sound of birds in the trees, wind whispering through leaves, and the raspy sound of her own breathing. She couldn't even hear his breathing.

She was alone out here in his fragrant, summer-scented garden, blindfolded, naked and vulnerable, on her hands and knees and bound to the low ceramic and wrought-iron table in the secluded arbor. Two years ago that might have made her panic, but not anymore. Tonight, he'd placed something new on her body, and the weight of it was as much a mark of his possession as anything else he'd given her—his collar around her neck, the rope he'd wound around her body and threaded through the O-ring, the weighted clamps he'd hung from her nipples—all of it part of the exquisite erotic torture he was so good at dishing out.

He hadn't stopped there tonight. Rope anchored her ponytail to…something. However, he had her trussed; she couldn't lower her head any farther than he'd allowed. Her knees were spread so wide she felt the warm summer air wafting over places she rarely felt it.

She was open to him in every way: mouth, pussy, ass. His toy to use as he saw fit. His toy to share. And he was going to share her tonight.

Her fantasy come to life, by virtue of his will.

She'd never been so aroused, so ready to scream and beg and plead for something to happen. For anything to happen. No one was touching her, no one was fucking her, but she poised on the edge of orgasm, though she wouldn't go over until she was given permission to do so.

The latch on the gate that led into the arbor made a soft snick as it was opened, followed by the scrape of shoes on the flagstone walk. She tensed slightly but forced herself to relax. She wanted this, but more importantly, he wanted this. What, when, where and how he wanted. He'd earned that right, proving himself over the past two years to be a Master she could trust.

A pair of hands landed on her hips and she jumped, as much as she was able to with the little slack he'd left her. Her heart started to pound. Another pair tugged lightly on the nipple clamps, and a fifth hand cupped her chin. Before she could process it all, a hard cock pushed into her wide-open mouth the same time as a thick plug breached her ass.

Her senses went wild and her mind went blank, turning her into a creature of nothing but sensation. The burn in her ass, the gagging as the cock in her mouth plunged deep, the fire in her nipples.

Then a voice in her ear as a flogger landed across her back once, twice, three times. His voice, both a whisper and a growl. "You look fucking gorgeous, angel. I can tell you want to come, but not until I say so."

The cock in her mouth withdrew, and she sucked in air. She panted as he stroked her ass, as he worked a finger inside her, around the plug. As her heart hammered, another cock plunged into her mouth. Her lips closed instinctively, but this wasn't him, either. She knew his taste, his smell, and this wasn't it. This cock was thinner than his, but longer. He, whoever he was, took quick strokes in and held them there for several long heartbeats. She counted in her head as he thrust again and again.

Her master's voice slid into her ear again as he rested his hand lightly on her neck. "I can feel him here, enjoying my toy, but you belong to me." His fingers loosened as the cock withdrew. "He's there only because I will it so, because it pleases me to see you being used."

Yes, she thought as she dragged more air in. She wanted to please him, more than anything else. Her pleasure came from his pleasure. She made a noise in the back of her throat, and he laughed, low and rough.

"Oh, we're not close to done yet, angel."

As the man fucked her mouth, another man fucked her ass with the plug. He pulled it out until the widest part of it stretched her, and then he slammed it in again. After a few times, he switched it for a thicker, vibrating plug. The man in her mouth and the man teasing her ass worked in unison, dragging her to the edge of madness over and over again to the point where she thought she might not be able to hold her orgasm, but easing off just before she flew off the cliff.

And then, suddenly, there was nothing.

She started to beg, desperate tears slipping from under her blindfold, her body aching with desire for him. "Please, Master. Please. I need to come. Please let me come. I need to come. Please, please, please. I need you. Oh, God. Fuck me, Master. Please."

Her arms and legs were released and then she was being turned onto her back, rose petals cushioning her. Their perfume exploded around her, mixing with the scent of her own arousal. His body stretched on top of hers, his cock nudging her entrance, but he held it there, not taking things any further, asserting his dominance. "My will, angel," he grunted. "You get what I choose to give to you, and all the begging in the world isn't going to sway me from that decision."

She whimpered, and he laughed softly, that Master's laugh that made her ache.

He released the blindfold and locked eyes with her, then buried himself deep inside her with one sharp thrust, his balls slapping against her ass. He fucked her hard, just the way she liked it. He made her scream, he made her beg for more, and then, when she could take no more, he gave her permission and made her come. As she pulsed around him, he spurted inside her, marking her as his.

When their breathing had calmed and she was able to focus, albeit dazedly, she blinked in the dim light, satisfied by the content look on his face. He tucked her head against his chest, stroking her back with his large, warm palm. The garden was empty now, except for the two of them. She didn't ask him who'd been here. She didn't want to know, and he probably wouldn't tell her. That was okay, because once again, he'd proven he was a master to trust. Not just now, but always. She looked down at the engagement ring he'd put on her finger at dinner tonight, right before he'd given her this.

His will, her fantasies. Their happily-ever-after.

Tell Me
By May Deva

"Oh, hell no!"

Diana strode into the room and threw the clothing at Marc. "No way, I am not doing a pinup shoot. I don't care what the bet was, or how long we've been friends!" She stood in front of him and glared at the camera he was fiddling with.

"Diana, a bet is a bet. Isn't that what you said? I've wanted to do this kind of shoot for ages. You've got a great look for it. Why fight it?" He smirked over the lens at her, knowing she'd never welsh.

"Shit. This sucks. I hate this kind of stuff. Couldn't we do something else?" She lowered her lashes, being coy.

"Nope. It's not my fault that you don't know when to fold, Di. And stop playing cute. I won't change my mind for a few bats of your eyelashes."

"Fuck you! To think I was worried you wanted me naked! This is worse." She grabbed the clothing, storming back to the change room.

Marc smiled. He knew she was bluffing last night, knew she didn't have the cards to beat him. Just like she was bluffing now. He wondered if she knew that she ran her tongue along the edge of her teeth when lying. Hopefully not, it was one of her quirks that brought his cock to attention. He fiddled with the lights, took some readings and waited.

"Ready, o demanding one!" Diana called as she sauntered into the studio. She saw Marc look up from the light meter he was holding and pause. She turned around slowly for effect. "Well?"

Marc realized he had been outdone. Diana stood in front of him, sporting her favorite over-the-knee striped socks and a white button down shirt held by a single button. Had she plumbed the depths of his fantasies, she couldn't have been more perfect.

"Um, Di? Isn't it a bit hot for—"

"This shirt? Totally." She popped the button and shrugged it off.

Marc swallowed, taking in the sheer black bikini panties that she revealed, breasts still hidden by her hair. "I was gonna say the socks, it being summer and all, but yeah, okay. You ready?" He turned away from her, using the movement to relieve some of the pressure building in his pants.

"You do realize that I'm not one of your little tarts who puts out for a good portfolio, right? How do I know if I'm ready? I've never done this before!" She put a hand on her hip and glared at him, just as the camera started to snap. "Wait, wait—I'm serious!" The lights made it hard to see his face. The camera kept snapping.

"Di, I keep telling you that you're a natural for this. Look at you, all huffy and hotter than hell. Those socks just wreck me. Turn a little to your left, yeah, a little more towards me. And Diana, use those lips for something other than talking, okay?"

She smirked and gave him the finger. Silence did prevail, the whir of the camera like punctuation in their thoughts. After some changes in position and attitude, she pulled a high stool into the light and leaned against it.

"Di?" His voice was quiet but rough, his arousal apparent. "Do you trust me?"

She drew a shaky breath, knowing where this could go. "I wouldn't be here otherwise."

"Lean back a bit, let the stool take some of your weight."

Placing her hands behind her on the sides on the stool, she flipped her hair over her shoulders and drew one foot up to rest on the rung. Canting her knee out, and leaning back, she asked, "Like this?"

His eyes flicked back and forth between her now bare breasts and the shadowed valley between her thighs. Somehow, those crazy socks were sexier than the finest stockings. The camera continued to snap.

Diana shifted slightly, bringing one hand forward and lightly skimming her fingertips across both nipples, bringing them to taut peaks. She slid her hand down the length of her body, dipping into her panties and slipping into her folds. Marc drew a breath. The sheer fabric hid nothing from him, and his cock twitched, growing harder.

"Like what you see?"

"Oh Di, so much. You've no idea."

"Don't I?" She leaned back further, tilting her hips to give herself better access. Circling her clit slowly, she grinned. "Then maybe you should come over here and show me."

He was at her side in a flash, replacing her hand with his own, dropping his head to nip at first one nipple then the other in turn. His touch was liquid heat, oozing through her and pooling at his fingertips as they slicked over and around every inch of her pussy. Arching into his hand, she pulled his lips to hers, nipping and sucking until they melded.

Diana moaned into his mouth as he slid two fingers slowly into her. His thumb set a circular rhythm on her clit; it wasn't long before he felt her body begin to tense. Breaking free of her mouth, he captured the closest nipple and sucked it between his lips, teeth and tongue providing just enough pleasure and pain to tip her over the edge. Her body rippled, flexed and then melted as the orgasm flowed through her and pulsed around his fingers. As her breathing slowed, her eyes found his and she smiled, reaching for his belt.

"Your turn."

"Can't, Di. My next client will be here in about five minutes. I should've timed this better."

"Well, how about later?"

"Absolutely." He leaned in and kissed her. "You owe me, vixen."

"Okay. So, let's say six at my place?" Slipping off the stool, she headed toward the change room.

"Perfect. I'll pick up Chinese?"

"Sure, that'd be great. Oh, Marc?"

He looked up.

"Last night? The final hand? I folded on a full house."

She ran her tongue across her teeth, grinned and let the door shut.

Summer Lightning
By Teresa Noelle Roberts

The beach started to clear out when dark thunderheads built up at the horizon and the wind picked up, churning the previously smooth, gentle surf into choppy mares of the sea, manes of spray blowing, but Pete and I decided we weren't ready to cut out yet. There was definitely a storm on the way, but we wanted to take a few minutes and enjoy the edged wind, tangy with salt and ozone and delicious after a sweaty day, and the wild surf.

The rain started gently enough, and with it, the trickle of people off the beach became a mass exodus. I snuggled closer to my husband as the rain came down. "Want to head back?" he asked, but it sounded like an automatic question.

"We're already in wet bathing suits. Why worry about it? We'll dry off at the cottage."

"And then get wet again, if I know you," Pete whispered in my ear.

"Right. Blame me."

"Who said anything about blaming?" We fell into a kiss, and he shielded me with his body from the passing mob as one hand caressed my nipple, making me shiver with pleasure at the touch itself and clench from knowing we were in public, even if no one was paying attention to much of anything other than heading back to the car before the heavens opened.

Pete's touch, and the hot, sweet kiss, and the cool rain on my hot skin made me feel more alive than I had in ages, more sensual, more grounded in my body.

And that was saying something. Ever since we'd arrived in Wellfleet three days ago, my sexuality and Pete's, all too long consigned to half-asleep weeknight fumblings or rushed, scheduled Saturday-morning-before-errands couplings had come back with a vengeance. I don't know if it was the ocean's inexorable rhythm, or the fresh air and sunshine, or the simple fact we were on vacation at last, but Pete and I had been acting more like young, randy honeymooners than a middle-aged couple who were coming up on twenty years together. The bed in our rented cottage had seen some serious action—as had the shower, the sofa, and, late on the first night, the screened-in porch. And at the rate we were going right there on the beach, we'd definitely work up an appetite for dinner the sexy way when we got back to the cottage. Hell, we were on the way already. Pete's hand had slipped inside my bikini top, and he was rolling my nipple between his thumb and forefinger. My hand was high on his thigh, inside the loose leg of his swimming suit, and if my palm wasn't on his cock yet, it was more due to a bad angle than any shyness on my part. We were kissing like kissing was the purpose of life. My blood pounded like the surf.

The rain picked up, slicking our skins but doing nothing to cool our ardor. Somewhere in the distance, a lifeguard with a megaphone announced that the beach was closing due to an approaching thunderstorm. "We should go," I muttered, reluctantly pulling myself away from Pete's arms. The sky looked darker now, ominous, and the ocean was roiling. Most of our fellow beachgoers had already cleared out, a few damp stragglers hauling coolers, chairs and kids toward the parking lots.

Pete moved as if to stand, then rolled back to me. "Got a better idea. Let's hang out and watch the storm."

It was the kind of thing we did twenty years ago. Ten years ago. Hell, even five years ago, before I started traveling so much for work and Pete got promoted. We'd enjoy the sunset together on the back porch, then go to bed early, or turn off the lights, open the windows and use a lightning storm as our personal special effects as we made love, or make naked snow angels in the dark yard, then run inside and warm each other. Not lately, though. Hell, this was the first vacation we'd taken in a few years— there'd been no time for more than the occasional long weekend. Even this vacation was a compromise; I had to call in to a meeting later in the week and Pete might have to go back to Boston for a day.

"Come back down here," I said, my voice throaty. And as Pete joined me again on the damp blanket, the first bolt of lightning lanced through the dark sky and struck the water. I jumped—right into Pete's arms.

I wasn't counting seconds, but by the time the thunder boomed, Pete had taken off my top, baring my breasts to the rain and his hands and tongue. The beach was empty by now except for us, but I'm not sure I'd have cared if it weren't. It felt so good to be naughty and playful as the rain fell and the lightning flashed. I was damp from the rain, but drenched from lust, and Pete's hot mouth sent snapping, sizzling bolts from my nipples to my clit.

As the rain stepped up, the storm drew closer, thunder rolling in right on the heels of the lightning. By that time, I'd worked Pete's trunks off, and he'd slithered me out of my bikini bottom. A rising tide brought the angry waves nearer to us, not close enough to be a threat, but enough to make us even more aware of the power of nature around us. We weren't taking time for finesse or drawn-out foreplay. It was all about our bodies crashing together as the thunder crashed overhead, as the waves crashed onto the shore. It was all about the thrill of the moment. All about each other, and recapturing a playful spontaneity we'd thought lost to time and maturity and "good" jobs.

Lightning crackled and danced across the dark, rain-swept sky, and thunder rattled us, and Pete drove hard inside me, bringing me closer to my own explosion of light and sound with each stroke. We were slick with rain, and wet sand infiltrated into places it didn't belong, but none of that mattered as much as Pete's cock in my cunt, Pete's arms sheltering me, my legs wrapped around Pete's hips, pulling him even deeper into me.

As orgasm overwhelmed me, I screwed my eyes shut, but I still sensed the brilliance of chain lightning through my closed lids, echoing the sensations roaring through my body. The clap of thunder, fierce overhead, drowned out Pete's guttural moan as he came.

Our storm passed before the one in the sky did. The temperature had dropped from the sultry heat of midday, and without Pete's body to warm me, and distraction of sex, I shivered. My bikini top had apparently washed out to sea, and my cover-up was a wet rag despite the scant protection of the beach bag. Pete grumbled as he pulled on his clammy trunks, and we rolled up the wet, sandy blanket as best we could.

But before we headed out, he pulled me close. "Look!" he exclaimed, pointing.

It was still pouring where we were, and thunder still rumbled in the distance. But a rainbow arched at the horizon, curving over the stormy sea.

"We did that," I joked. "Now let's go take a hot shower…and then we'll see if we can make another one."

To Hell with Sunset
By A.M. Hartnett

I clung to the stern of the Dawny Beth. Stern? Bow? Or was it stem? The ass end. Whatever it was called, it was the only thing that was going to keep me from going overboard when I came.

Well, almost the only thing. I was going to have to trust that Captain Zach's grip on my hips would keep me from going headfirst into Xavier's Bay. He dug in hard enough that I'd have to explain the bruises on my hips tomorrow.

In the meantime, I was going to focus on that tongue.

Zach had taken the boat far enough that the shore and rolling hills beyond looked smudged and surreal. At my back was the sunset I had been so desperate to see. I hadn't been able to recruit any of the other cottage-dwellers for this evening excursion, and so I took my Alberta-born, ocean-starved, landlocked ass to the wharf to buy a ticket on my own. The touring company didn't do evening cruises unless by appointment, I found out, and only in groups. Zach had heard my curse. He had a boat that smelled like the lobster traps he was repairing that afternoon. He offered me a private cruise, no charge, and even shared his beer with me.

I liked his quasi-Irish East coast accent. I liked his big arms and tanned hands. I liked that he'd invited me into the wheelhouse to steer the boat as an excuse to make his move. I liked that his hands were rough on my belly while he unbuttoned my shorts.

Oh, and I really liked that he looked up at me the whole time he ate my pussy.

I kept my head lowered, locked in that brown-eyed gaze as he flicked the tip of his tongue in a half-moon along the underside of my clit. He was just teasing me for now. I could see it in the way his eyes lit up each time I twitched and gasped. I wanted more, and he wanted to play with me.

I wasn't getting anywhere by begging. He was the captain, so he got his way. I waited, writhing and whimpering as he toyed with me. I was dying. Dying. I wanted that hot tongue to make me come.

He drew back, his wet mouth in a grin and his gaze never breaking with mine as he pulled the hood taut around my clit. He flattened out his tongue and so slowly, so fucking sinfully, licked my pussy from top to bottom.

Or stem to stern, if you want to get thematic about it.

The sun could have exploded across the sky and I wouldn't have paid any attention. I couldn't tell which was the water sloshing against the boat and which was the wet sound of his tongue lapping me. As he bobbed his head, dragging his tongue back and forth, I rocked my ass in time with him.

"Fuck—oh, fuck, like that."

I released my grip on the boat and grasped two fistfuls of hair. If I fell in, fine, as long as it was when that wicked tongue was done with me.

He drew back abruptly, and I actually growled and tried to shove his face back in my crotch. He dragged my hands away from his head and stood, then turned me around.

"Sorry, I can't wait any longer," he muttered, and pushed down at the small of my back. My ass went up.

"Do you do this with all the tourists?" I asked as I waited for him to slip on a condom.

"Nope, you're the first."

He could have been lying. He probably was lying, but I didn't care.

The sun was in front of me now, a fireball set against streaks of violet and gold. I bowed before it. I had come to take pictures, but as his cock stretched me I knew I wouldn't need a picture. This sunset would be burned into my brain for eternity.

One hand wrapped around me, and his fingers picked up where his tongue left off. With the other hand, he grabbed hold of my ponytail, "for your own good, so you don't fall," and pumped me steady and solid. I was going to leave scratches in the wood beneath my fingers if I gripped it any tighter.

Big blue ocean. Sun setting. Shorts around my ankles. A hard belly slapping my ass. Grinding into his rough fingers.

And, oh fuck, that sting in my scalp every time he tugged my hair.

Could I have gotten a better cruise than this? I think not.

He was practically silent as he pounded me, save for the occasional grunt, but I couldn't keep my mouth shut. I'm sure the wind picked up my moans and carried them to shore. I'm sure somewhere around Xavier Bay, someone heard me begging for a harder fuck. Someone heard me get the harder fuck I asked for, and a juicy orgasm. As my clit throbbed under his fingers and my cunt squeezed around his dick, Zach yanked my head back and used his grip on me as leverage.

Stem, stern, bow, whatever. The edge jabbed my thighs as he pushed me forward and pounded me to his own unrelenting finish.

The first thing I saw when the splotches in my vision cleared was a star. An actual star. There was a violet glow on the waterline that bled into the indigo sky.

"I missed my sunset," I said breathlessly, and shivered as he withdrew his shrinking cock.

He wrapped his thick arms around my middle and rested his forehead on my shoulder as we both worked for air. "I've got a view of the bay from my deck. How about watching the sunrise? You'll probably still be awake anyway."

The Chaperone
By Primula Bond

The idea of swinging in a hammock above the Bay of Naples seemed like heaven when my cousin suggested it.

"How's the love life?" Samantha asked as we washed our hands in the ladies' loo of the pub.

"Dry as lava dust."

"So come to Amalfi! Paid for by the agency. Sizzling sun. Cartloads of culture."

Me and two budding nineteen-year-old supermodels shaking their booty like the Cheeky Girls. I caught sight of my reflection in the tarnished mirror. Hair falling out of a topknot, eyes shadowy over my emerald pashmina. Not so much cheeky as peaky.

"The agency will only let us have a break if we take —"

"Minder?"

Sam giggled. "Chaperone. To stop us ruining our looks for the winter shoots."

Swinging in a hammock over the Bay of Naples with a pair of honeys was looking like utter madness.

###

The villa was paradise on a pink cliff. But my girls were getting restless.

"That's smoke from the forest fires," murmured Sam, fanning herself with my newspaper.

Greta stood up, twitching a shiny triangle of pink thong. Her blonde hair was cropped like a boy's, unlike mine and Sam's, which is untamed ringlets. "Let's go to the beach."

The cove was deserted apart from a couple of divers wading out of the sea. One was tall and dark with a wetsuit rolled down over a ridged brown torso.

The other wore a pair of faded denim shorts and was the color of golden syrup. He shook his bleached hair like a Labrador.

Sam and Greta went into slinky catwalk mode, tilting their chins as they passed.

"Remember your duties!" said Sam, snatching the cream and kneeling behind Greta. "Got to keep the sun off."

She smoothed the cream onto Greta's back, hands trailing round to her breasts. The barman tipped beer into his mouth and massaged the front of his shorts.

His diver mate started to peel off his wetsuit. Hair ran down his stomach into his groin. He'd never imagine I was lusting after him. I was invisible beside the girls and I decided to leave them to it.

The coach swayed round the winding coast road. The sky was smudged gray with smoke. I glanced back at the cliffs, where my hungover girls lay in their stifling room. Earlier I'd found Greta straddling Sam as the sheet slipped off.

I trailed through the sizzling heat in Pompeii, through the ruined shops and houses, along the narrow streets where chariots used to race.

"And this was a bordello," said a tour guide as I wandered into a warren of tiny chambers. "Those were beds where they pleasured their clients."

I leaned against the wall, limp with frustration.

"The blonde lady from the beach."

A white shirtsleeve blocked my way out.

"I'm her cousin." My body was licked by fire. "What are you doing here?"

"Tourist guide. And you're the cousin I want." He was so close that the hardness of his cock shoved through his trousers. Excitement shot up my legs.

"What did you say this place was?" His maleness pulsed into the cooked air.

"The *lupanare*. The frescoes should give you a clue."

Faint figures in terracotta and black hovered over the ancient bricks. They weren't dancing or praying. They were copulating in every position under the sun. Here was a man fucking a slender girl from behind. A woman with coiled elegant hair straddled a man as he reclined on cushions.

"It's like a menu. All the services you could get for your *dinarii*."

Another pair went at it face-to-face, togas slipping to the floor. A tart lowered her face into her client's groin.

"Were they in here when the lava came?" Imagine giving pleasure, selling your aching pussy for money before you die. "Were they, you know, *in flagrante?*"

"Some of them, yes. But what a way to go." He started to lift my silky dress. "Coming to your favorite tart, fucking her senseless, not a clue what's happening outside these walls, just lost inside her, pumping your life away."

He ran his fingers under my dress and lifted me. My pussy moistened as my dress floated round my waist. My breasts bulged honey-dark in the half-light.

Footsteps scraped in the dust outside. The diver slammed me against the wall.

"Safe inside the *lupanere*. Everyone fucking like there's no tomorrow."

I couldn't tell if it was sweat or I was creaming myself. I opened myself wider as I wound my fingers in his hair to smother him between my damp breasts.

His fingers released my musky scent. His teeth tore my flimsy dress. Suddenly, there were voices in the doorway, the click of a camera, a gasp. Our eyes glittered in the suffocating gloom of our hot whorehouse.

He swore. "I have to join my group!"

"Fuck your group."

I barely felt the scratch of stone as he reared over me like one of the men in the etchings. There was his prick and my legs were hooking him in.

How tiny those Pompeiians must have been. Our bodies were stuck as his cock slid inside. He squeezed my breasts, pinching my nipples as he bit my neck, pausing to listen, and then we were rocking together, his cock filling me totally.

Voices shouted. Coaches sounded their horns as he fucked me. A siren wailed up over Naples and a helicopter whirred overhead. My lover groaned again, and the thought of the volcano and the fires drove my excitement until he shuddered and I came, too.

We staggered out of the *lupanere* and back through the ruined town.

The sky was a venomous yellow and there was a scorching in the air.

"I'll meet you on the beach," my lover called as my bus rumbled back towards the coast.

Hot as Ice
By Sammi Lou Thorne

After doing yardwork for most of the morning, I was exhausted.

Wiping off my sweaty forehead with the back of my wrist, I sat down on the steps to take a break. I used my hand to shade my eyes from the hot sun as I surveyed the yard with its freshly cut grass.

The door opened and closed behind me. "You look hot," said Will, my husband, as he bent over to kiss my neck. "And you taste salty."

I laughed. "I'm sweating like crazy. I should have waited until later in the day to get this done."

He sat down next to me and handed me a tall glass of water packed with ice. The ice cubes clicked together as I took several long swallows.

"Thanks," I said. "Now I just need to take a shower and cool off."

He gently pushed me back into the steps. "I've got a better idea to cool you off." He reached into my nearly empty glass, extracted an ice cube, and sucked it into his mouth. I looked up at him and laughed.

"What are you going to do with that?"

He didn't answer; instead, he bent over me and kissed me, teasing my lips open. The ice was cold and wet, and it slipped easily back and forth between our mouths and thrusting tongues, melted droplets sliding down my throat. I could feel myself becoming aroused and wet, and my nipples began to harden, poking against my shirt.

When the ice cube had melted completely, Will pulled back. "You really should get out of those sweaty clothes," he said.

I didn't hesitate—I sat up and pulled off my tank top. My breasts glistened with a sheen of sweat. Removing my tennis shoes and socks, I stood up. Will was getting turned on, and I could see his cock straining against his shorts. I slowly unzipped my denim shorts, letting them fall to the hot cement. My panties followed. Naked, I stepped onto the grass and then sat down, feeling the freshly cut blades of grass tickle my legs. Lying back onto my elbows with my legs out in front of me, I watched Will walk over to me, his fingers dipping into the glass he still held in his hand.

He sat next to me, facing me, and set the glass down within reach.

He held up an ice cube from the glass. A few drops fell from it onto the hollow of my neck, running slowly down into the cleft between my breasts. He took the ice and placed it on my nipple, making me jump.

"That's cold!" I exclaimed, and he smiled.

"What better way to cool down?" he asked, rubbing the ice on my chest, leaving trails of water behind. He took a second piece of ice and traced circles with the cubes on my breasts, making my nipples cold and taut in the hot air. I moaned with pleasure.

When the ice had melted, Will got a fresh cube and placed it in his mouth. I thought he was going to kiss me, but instead he leaned forward, grasped my breast with his hand, and pulled my nipple into his mouth while using his other hand to tweak and tease my free nipple. As he gently sucked, he rolled his tongue and the piece of ice around, teasing me. As my nipple grew colder from the ice, I felt a flood of wetness between my legs and my pussy tingled with anticipation. I closed my eyes and savored the sensation.

Will's mouth and hands and hands left my breasts, and I heard him retrieve another ice cube from the glass. I opened my eyes and watched as he took the ice and touched it to my skin. He ran it slowly down from between my breasts to my navel. Its cool caress made me shiver. As water began to pool in my belly button, I spread my legs and Will moved between them. He moved the ice slowly downward, and I shivered in anticipation. The ice was almost gone, but he moved the small sliver that was left downward, and I jumped when it touched my clit.

He took another ice cube and put it in his mouth, and I moaned as he nestled his head between my legs. He spread my shaven lips with his fingers, and when his cold, wet tongue touched my protruding clit, I nearly came. I was awash in pleasure as he lapped at my clit, circling it with his tongue and then pushing the ice cube over and around it. Holding the ice on my clit with his tongue, he began gently sucking. I threw my head back and lost myself in the feeling, the cold sending delicious chills up my body.

Several pieces of ice melted between my clit and his mouth, and I was on the edge. With the last piece of ice in his mouth, he teased my throbbing clit before using his tongue to push the ice inside my pussy.

I came hard, my moans becoming screams as my orgasm washed over me. My warm juices flooded over his tongue and into his mouth, melting the last of the ice.

When my tremors subsided, I raised my head and looked down at Will through half-closed eyes. "My God, that was fantastic," I said. He rose up and scooted next to me, kissing me long and deep.

"I hope that cooled you down some," he said.

I grinned at him. "I think it made me hotter."

"In that case," said Will, "I better go get some more ice."

Protection
By Elise Hepner

There was a splash near the side of my head, but I didn't bother looking into the glaring sun as heat twinkled behind my closed eyelids. I snuggled closer into the warming plastic. I'd been out here long enough for my husband to come bother me for being a sloth, but I couldn't break the spell that the calming humidity wrapped around my flesh like an invisible leash.

"Have you redone your sunscreen?" Jordan whispered in my ear, voice lazy and low in the ways that brought my brain to an abrupt halt. The small amount of pressure he exerted with the ropey muscles of his forearms against the plastic made my whole body sway as the raft listed to one side. Even with my eyes closed, awareness of his whole body blasted through my every cell. "Permission to come aboard?"

There wasn't enough room for both of us. A little noise of surprise fell from my lips before his muscled weight pressed tight and hot from between my legs and all the way up against my chest. His dusky head of hair whispered against my shoulder, lips brushing against my tender collarbone—where he'd bitten me only the other night, skin still hyper sensitive. Small drops of water trickled along my stomach and the line of my hips beneath my bikini bottom. My fingers twisted in the plastic armrests, and I tried to remain still so I wouldn't go plunging into the lukewarm water. His slow laughter rolled goose bumps down my arms until the sun tingled on my skin, plucking moisture while I did my best to ignore the wicked heat between my legs.

"If you can be lazy all day, you can lay here while I do other things. The sun may put you to sleep like a cat, but I'll wake up your pussy."

While I fought the urge to fidget, Jordan's wicked fast fingers plucked at the small strings on my bikini until the fabric fell free from my hips. I peeked through my lashes, his head a halo blocking out the sun. And I held my breath meeting his electric gaze while he threaded his fingers between our linked bodies and palmed my half-naked cunt. A whisper of a groan breathed across my lips until the act of breathing became a tease. Meanwhle, my husband's fingers dragged away the material from underneath me, forcing me to gently lift up my ass so we didn't tip over.

Warm water kissed the edge of my thigh, and I swallowed past the tightness in my throat. The strings of my swimsuit were mere wisps across my upper body as Jordan drew my bottoms up the line of my half-naked body. The heat trapped from his erection beneath his board shorts pressed tight between my thighs, and I wanted to taste him on my lips.

"What game are you playing?"

"Put your arms overhead."

"We'll tip."

"Don't tell me you don't like the edge." His fierce tone made my next sentence snag, and I did what he asked without another question. A slow roll of my wrists above my head. Every inch I stretched out placed our bodies firmly against each other until I trembled despite the heat.

The slightly damp fabric knotted around my wrists until my arms were bound together. I fought not to wrap my legs around his hips to complete my submission. But he knew—by the way his pelvis ground into me while his tongue trailed smooth circles against the side of my neck—he knew every little movement or protest I wanted to make before I dared to move an inch. His knowledge was like paralysis while he continued to experiment along my subtle curves. A tweak, a pulse, a brush, and a slap. Sensations woke up my drowsy senses, forcing me into the present while his fingers and mouth explored his personal playground. My pulse shifted down toward my curled toes. His low verbal taunts whispered from neck to nipple with the threat of teeth, and his callused fingers broke my summer slump into a million ecstatic pieces.

I pulsed around the forceful, unforgiving girth of his fingertips, yearning for my knot of pleasure to tighten until I was caught up by lust. Bliss swept in waves. But I kept my prone position, barely a wiggle or a whimper to break my inaction and deny his dominance. Our precarious balance thrummed in my fingertips. My inner wrists flirted together, light brushstrokes of pleasure with my swimsuit keeping me in check, and his fingers continued his rough strokes echoing the laps of the water against the gentle rock of our raft.

Even in a floating chair made for one—Jordan made the plastic and foam his throne. And through the cusp of my orgasm I was crowned consort, chest aching through every heated breath. My breasts strained against what little was left of my bikini top after he'd dragged it down past my nipples.

Summer—and his use of my body—was payment for the sweet, mind-melting break that Jordan only tolerated with his inability to be inactive. My slick come was as good as any rent check. Stolen moans as precious as a load of done dishes. And the pursuit of laziness was etched into my bones and across my pale flesh.

The raft dipped, we spasmed, and I held my breath. With bonds slick and tight, I sliced into the pool that Jordan billed me for through late-night blowjobs and afternoon fucks on our covered porch.

And it was the best money ever spent.

An Oven on Broil
By Tenille Brown

"It's too hot to do any damn thing."

Louise was talking to herself more than anyone else, especially since she was the only one there.

She wasn't about to turn on the stove in this heat, so she was making a salad for dinner. It was hotter than it should have been in October, and Louise had gotten fed up standing at the kitchen counter tearing lettuce.

Doug would fuss about her running the air conditioner, but Louise didn't care. He should have been home fixing her car anyway. Instead, he was in town running his mouth with his friends.

Louise had started on the tomatoes when the unit went out. It made a sort of hum and moan and all of a sudden it felt like someone had cut on the oven and set it on broil.

Louise stopped chopping and called Doug.

She tried him five times, dialing and fanning before she decided to just go down and get him.

The walk was hot, and Louise was getting madder by the yard.

It only took her eighteen minutes to cover two miles, and she had worked up a sweat by the time she got there, makeup running down her face.

She saw Doug's back first, wide and chiseled in his snug shirt. He was leaned against his truck, tall glass of ice water in his hand.

Instead of calling his name to get his attention, Louise walked up behind him and poked him hard on the shoulder.

"The air conditioning went out," she said when he turned to face her.

"You don't need air conditioning in October anyway."

"But I do need my car fixed, which is why I had to walk to tell you about the air."

Doug's buddies were staring at them, Louise with both hands on her hips, Doug scratching his head full of thick, dark hair.

He walked around to the driver's side.

"Come on. I'll take a look at the unit."

Louise got in, but opted to lean against the door instead of shoulder to shoulder close to him like she normally would.

He handed her his glass of water.

Louise took it and sipped.

The air was on full blast, and Louise was thankful for the hard burst of chill from the vent. She leaned back, closing her eyes and she almost forgot, just for a second, how mad she was.

Then Doug reached over and touched her thigh which made her jump, spilling the cold water all over her lap.

"Goddamn it, Doug!"

"I didn't mean it, Lou, geez."

He grabbed a handful of napkins from the glove compartment and began patting at the wetness where her yellow sundress was now sticking to her.

He didn't move his hand when he was done.

"You sure are hot, Lou."

"Hmph. You think?"

"And I know I owe you one."

He was rubbing now and squeezing and Louise knew just what Doug had on his mind. He couldn't help it. He got his rocks off of seeing her mad, and it didn't help matters that what she was wearing was now see-through after being saturated with water.

Louise looked at her husband out of the corner of her eye as he casually turned their pickup down a dirt road. He drove half the way down before he stopped and put it in park.

"Get out."

Louise didn't know when her frown curled into a smile. All she knew was that they were both climbing out of the truck, and then they were leaning against it.

Doug's hands were on Louise's thighs again, massaging.

"In case your legs are sore from the walk."

"They're not."

In fact, they were weakening and trembling, and Doug's hand was moving further up, pulling Louise's dress up along with it, exposing the smooth brown legs and hips beneath.

Doug flicked his tongue against Louise's ear.

"Are you still mad?"

"Not as much."

How could she be with him touching her like that? With him tugging at her panties and rubbing his forefinger against her clit?

She heard the delicate fabric of her panties ripping just as Doug pinned her against the truck, his lips running kisses over her neck and shoulders, his hands holding her at the waist.

"On the back of the truck?" he asked.

"As good a place as any."

Louise didn't care that there were no sheets or blankets there. She just wanted him inside her. She was willing to risk a few minutes of discomfort for some spontaneous fucking in the middle of a hot day.

Doug guided Louise to the back of the truck and eased her on her back. Her dress was rolled up to her breasts now and the hot ridges of the truck bed stung her skin.

She flinched.

Doug paused.

"Too hot?"

Louise shook her head and pulled Doug closer.

"No, keep going."

Doug worked his way out of his shorts, exposing a lengthy and solid cocoa cock that he placed directly between her legs as he lowered himself inside her.

It was like someone stuck a fork in her. Louise wouldn't last a minute, not if Doug kept on like this.

His moves were fluid. His humming in her ear didn't help matters. She was turned on high, and she couldn't help it. She was going to boil over.

She clutched his cheeks, moved her fingers to the middle of his ass. He moved faster, harder.

I can come before I burn…I can come before I burn…I can…

Louise clenched her thighs tighter, but it worked against her.

"Doug!"

His name left her lips in one staggered syllable. She held him in place mid-thrust and came with everything she had in her.

Doug whispered in her ear, "I'll call them in the morning, first thing, I promise."

And Louise nodded, "That's fine, baby."

Summer in December
By Tamsin Flowers

Call me a stickler for tradition but when it's summer on the calendar, I like hot, and when it says winter, I want snow. Which is just one of the reasons why I should never have taken a job as second chef at an Antarctic research station. Yes, sure, there was snow in winter. But it wasn't hot in summer, it was cold, and it wasn't summer in July, it was summer in December. And when it should have been summer it was winter and even colder. Doing your head in? I live here and I can't get my head around it.

And the other reason why I shouldn't have taken the job? Al, the delectable head chef and my boss, who sees me as nothing more than the girl who peels, chops and mashes the potatoes. But then I didn't know about Al when I took the job.

Between the two of us, we prep three meals a day for the thirty-five scientists that work at the research station, seven days a week, in two month rotations. If you've ever worked a kitchen, you'll know how hot and intense things get. But if you work a kitchen with a guy who you can't get out of your mind at the end of the shift, who you want to fuck senseless on the steel countertops and suck off in the walk-in cold store? It's a whole lot hotter and a whole lot more intense.

But Al doesn't see me that way. So I have to go into the cold store on my own to pour water on the flames. I do that by working out how many potatoes I will have peeled by my next home leave.

Apart from Al and myself, the scientists are all Australian, so they get the summer in December thing. But being weirded out by the seasons, that's the one thing Al and I have in common. Like today: It's December twenty-first, the summer solstice. It won't even get dark, but it's still as cold as fuck. The scientists have all gone on a two-day expedition, so it's only me and Al, having an easy day, quietly preparing things for the week ahead. I know this is my one chance, so when Al suggests taking the evening off...

"What's this?" says Al, when I put a glass down beside his computer, where he's still working.

"Piña colada. It's midsummer, so we're going to the beach."

He gives me the sort of look generally reserved for pesky younger sisters.

"Taste it," I say.

Two words irresistible to a chef.

Down on the beach, we kick snow into the water and Al suggests building a snowman rather than a sandcastle. I know he's humoring me now, wondering how long he has to stay here before going back to his work. I watch him running along the edge of the water. So hot with his dark jeans carelessly crumpled at the top of his snow boots, his narrow hips looking even narrower below the bulk of his down jacket. The wind ruffles his black hair, his cheeks so rosy with cold that I want to lick them warm. I desperately need him to notice me as something more than a potato-processing drone.

It's now or never.

"I'm going for a dip," I yell, when he's at the other end of the small, curved cove above which the research station sits.

If this doesn't make him sit up and notice, nothing will.

I shed my parka, kick off my boots and slide out of my pants. I didn't bring a bikini, so I'm wearing my most presentable matching underwear. I know it's going to hurt like hell when I take the plunge, so I can't afford to pussyfoot at the edge.

I take a low, horizontal dive into the water.

Holy fuck!

My skin is burning. My fingers and toes are pain like nothing on this earth. My teeth chatter like a pneumatic drill's going off in my skull. Someone's rubbing warm hands up and down one of my calves, massaging my foot. Someone's talking to me.

"Can you hear me now? Andi, can you hear me?"

I think I nod but I can't really feel my body.

"What the fuck were you thinking? You nearly killed yourself."

I've never heard Al this angry, even when I ruined a whole day's work by putting the oven on extra high instead of low.

"I'm okay," I say but all I hear is chattering teeth and spluttering noises.

I'm wrapped in a fleecy blanket, and I look around. We're in a bedroom, and it isn't mine. It must be Al's. Underneath the blanket, I realize I'm naked. I see my underwear in a pool of water on the floor.

My whole body's trembling and shaking. Any deliberate movement is completely beyond my control.

"Jesus, I've gotta get you warmed up fast," says Al.

I'm naked on his bed. I have ideas about getting warm. At least my brain does; I'm not sure my body is quite there.

"Sh-sh-sh-shared b-b-body heat," I manage through my teeth.

It's true—it works. It's what they tell you to do in the safety manuals. It was simply a sensible suggestion that could save my life. It had nothing to do with the thought of Al having to get naked, too, and press his hot body against the length of my cold one.

His look says that he knows exactly what I'm playing at.

Silently, he strips off his clothes and joins me on the bed, pulling the fleecy blanket around us and the rest of the bed covers up as far as our shoulders. He smells good in the confined space. Yes, a little sweaty. After all, he did have to pick me up and carry me up the shore and into the station, him fully dressed in a 750 fill power down jacket. But spicy and masculine in a way that makes me want suck the air around him and drink it up.

I press myself against him and this, I think, is when I finally breach his defenses. He lets out a long, low moan and wraps his arms tight around me. His body feels red hot in comparison to mine and, hell, I want to stay just pressed against him like this forever.

"You didn't need to do that to get my attention. You had it from the get go."

I put both my trembling hands up to his cheeks and look deep into his chestnut eyes. I have to wonder if I'm delirious from the cold shock. But he's smiling at me and there's a hunger in his expression. A hunger for me.

"Your mouth looks cold," he whispers.

His lips on mine feel like a hot brand, and his tongue touches mine like warm velvet. My hips respond by bucking against him, and he slides a hand to the small of my back to press me steadily into him. I can feel his cock, hot and hard, against my stomach. I murmur my appreciation and put a hand down to feel it.

"Fuck! Your hands are like ice," he says.

Slowly, he sucks each of my fingers to bring them back to life. I'm experiencing an extraordinary combination: My skin burns as he warms each cold centimeter of me, while inside I'm melting with desire, so ready for what I know is coming.

"I'm sorry, Al," I say. "I needed you to see me. I need you to fuck me."

He stops sucking my fingers and slides a hand up between my thighs. Blissful warmth floods through me.

"Oh God, I've wanted to. So much," he says. "But..."

"What?" I whisper, placing a warmer hand on his cock. It twitches at my touch, surging forward against my palm.

"We work together..."

Two fingers slide inside me, exploring just about the only part of me that's warm. I let my legs go slack and they fall wide open. An invitation. Al pulls his fingers out, and I feel his cock nudging its way into me. He's slow and gentle, sending a cascade of shivers up and down my spine as my pussy clenches and unclenches, pulsing against him. A sigh, a whimper and then I feel his mouth on one of my breasts. Soft, warm suction sends heat flaring through my chest.

Now I'm warm. Now I'm being fucked by Al, hard and fast in the way that I'd dreamt he would. The embers that have been glowing for so long, deep down inside me catch alight. The slow-growing fire blazes up as the heat of my climax builds within me. Al is pounding hard into me, creating glorious, hot friction, burning me from the inside. Our sweat mingles as our bodies clash, and I feel his back stiffen. He lets out a harsh grunt as he comes inside me.

His cock pulses, and I feel the hot discharge of his semen flooding me. It pushes me over the edge, and my own orgasm flares, flashing though me, making me gasp.

"Happy summer," Al whispers, as we lie together, panting as the sweat dries on our bodies.

"Four days till Christmas," I say.

Splash
By Kathleen Delaney-Adams

Steamy August nights will always remind her of him. The way the humid, evening air cleaves to her skin, thick like longing, heavy with anticipation. The way the buzzing of the cicadas resonates inside her veins, throbbing and humming with electricity, a rhythm she will forever associate with him.

He pulled up to The Amsterdam on his bike, and her pussy was already slick. Delilah had been waiting for him for hours, dancing herself into a sweat in the packed club, waiting for his arrival. She sipped frothy pink cocktails and laughed with her friends, all the while keeping one heavily mascara-d eye on the door.

Von swaggered in, the sort of walk that makes a girl want to fall over onto her back and spread her legs wide open. He made Delilah breathless, breathless and wet. He was a salt-and-pepper butch, her favorite kind. His confidence spoke volumes of experience, and Delilah longed to discover exactly what kind of experience he had.

Tonight was by all technicalities their second "date," the first taking place spontaneously during a poetry event. As soon as Von called to tell her he would pick her up on his bike and take her home, she had slipped into the bathroom and removed her panties. She slid a finger into her cunt to inspect. Slick and creamy, just as he had instructed.

Von's eyes caught hers from her advantageous door-viewing spot at the bar. Delilah attempted to saunter casually across the room, but ended up dashing to his side and grabbing his arm, breathless with excitement. Von laughed approvingly at her obvious enthusiasm. He slung an arm around her waist, drawing her to him.

"Ready?"

"Always." She flirted up at him.

Von steered her through the hopping, gyrating crowd, one hand on the flat of her back, just the way Delilah liked it. Once outside, the moist air teased her already heated flesh. Oh, this was going to be a good night, she could just tell.

They stopped at his bike, and Von grabbed Delilah's hair in one hand, twining it between his fingers and pulling her head back. She uttered a soft gasp of pain before his mouth was on hers, sampling her greedily. His lips devoured hers, and Delilah struggled for a moment, resisting, fear and longing wrestling inside her. Lust won out, and she melted against him, her hands on his chest. His tongue demanded and took, and she could only acquiesce, willingly answering his hunger with her own.

His hands roved over her body, exploring every inch, learning her curves and the softness of her skin. She sighed into him, inviting him, accessible and pliant as he groped at her flesh. His thumbs found Delilah's breasts and rubbed them through the sheer fabric of her dress. She shivered in response. He pinched and pulled at her erect nipples, twisting them until she cried out. Abruptly, he stepped back and studied her a moment.

"Are you sure you are ready to take this on?" he asked.

Delilah surprised them both by closing the distance between them and grabbing his rubber cock in one hand, squeezing it gently. Mmm. How she loved a butch that packed. When Von responded by groaning and closing his eyes, she applied more pressure, tugging and rubbing him through his jeans. She thrilled when he strained and swelled at her insistent touch. Yum.

"Oh, I'm ready," she purred up at him.

Von wrapped his hands around her waist and turned her roughly, bending her over the seat of his bike. Her arms flailed for something to hold on to but found nothing. She dangled helplessly over his bike as he yanked her dress up over her ass, exposing her pussy to him. He nodded, satisfied with what he saw, then kicked her legs apart with his boot, allowing even greater access to her cunt.

Without warning, he shoved three fingers inside her, then four, pumping into her tight hole. She was so wet for him she opened easily. She writhed and struggled, taking him in, hips rocking against him, moaning in need. She cried out as he fucked her with his fingers, her hunger and pain so great she wondered how she was still standing. Liquid fire in her tummy, her cunt, consumed her and demanded release. He pulled his fingers out and she boiled over, splashing onto the engine of his bike.

Von stepped back from her, panting and taking in every inch of her. Unaware of how gorgeous she looked, Delilah lay, spread legged and quivering, over his soaked bike.

She breathed in deeply, welcoming the summer breeze perfumed with jasmine, the call of the cicadas answering her own wild cry. She threw back her head and laughed into the August night.

Hot Tomato
By Thomas S. Roche

Ever since it got hot this summer, you've started gardening wearing almost nothing. A long T-shirt with no pants; the one-piece you wear to swim; shorts with no top; sometimes just your bra and panties. Once I caught you gardening naked, and that made you blush. You always wash yourself off with the garden hose before you come back inside, dripping on the floor, your skin steamy with the heat and the moisture. Recently, your arms have been bundled with zucchini, squash, carrots.

Now, it's finally tomato season.

You've got on your red string bikini, the one you wear to sunbathe. There's not much to it; it's nothing more than a string between your cheeks, and in the front it hangs so low I can see a hint of your pubic hair. If you wore it outside the backyard, you'd have to shave, I think. On top it clings to your breasts awkwardly, looking like at any moment it's going to fall away into nothing. It's bright red. Tomato red.

I watch you from the patio, reclining on a chaise longue with an ice-cold Bloody Mary. I watch you on your hands and knees, checking tomatoes and picking the ones that are ripe. Picking up snails by the shell and tossing them indelicately over the fence into the neighbor's yard. Bending far forward, so far forward that I can see the lips of your sex spreading around the thin string of your bikini bottoms. So far forward that I can see your upper body from between your legs, your nipples popping out of the bikini top as you pluck a tomato from a plant. I lick the vodka-and-Tabasco-spiked tomato taste from a celery stalk and wonder if your pussy tastes like tomatoes when you've been picking them all day.

You straighten, bundling the fruits of your labor in your arms awkwardly, reaching behind you to pluck the string from between your cheeks, perhaps not even realizing that I could see your lips. You adjust the top, tucking your nipples away. The bright red bikini contrasts against your rich, tanned skin. I start to get hard.

You come back toward the house with your arms filled with tomatoes, pausing only to turn on the garden hose and spray water over your muddy knees and feet, washing them clean so that your tanned skin glistens. Water splashes up and moistens your bikini top, making it even more transparent, making it cling more firmly to the shape of you. Your face is a mask of elation, your eyes bright with enthusiasm as you rush toward the kitchen.

"*Wait* until you taste these *tomatoes*," you gush.

My eyes linger on your full, ripe breasts, nipples distending the red material of your top. I smile at you.

"I can hardly wait," I say.

You disappear into the kitchen, your cheeks bouncing ripe as I glance back after you. I have to readjust my shorts to keep my cock from pressing painfully against them. I sip the Bloody Mary and taste the sharp vodka and hot sauce camouflaging the taste of tomato.

You come out a few minutes later with the cutting board, ripe tomatoes sliced and laid out. You're also holding glass of water. "You *have* to try these," you say, your breasts almost popping out of your bikini top as you come around and kneel by my chaise longue.

"I want to try them," I say.

"Here," you tell me, handing me the water. "Clean your palate. Swish it around. You've got to have a clean palate."

"My palate is anything but clean," I say.

"I know. Drink the water."

I drink half the glass and swish the water around my mouth, washing away the taste of the Bloody Mary.

"Now close your eyes," you tell me.

I close them and open my mouth.

"Just taste," you say, and place a tomato slice on my tongue like a bikini-clad priest disbursing the Holy Communion.

The tomato is still hot from the sun. The taste is hearty, rich. The bite of citrus is followed by a rush of smoky taste—pure musk.

"Doesn't it just taste like sex?" you giggle.

I open my eyes, look into yours, and let my glance flicker down over your body, its ripe rounded curves full and pink with the sun.

"Yes," I say. "It tastes exactly like sex."

"Okay," you say. "Here, drink more water and close your eyes."

I obey, opening my mouth.

"This is a different variety," you tell me. "This is an heirloom."

"You don't say."

This one, also warm, is faintly spicy, the taste pulsing hot through my tongue before the musky bouquet hits me. It's spicy enough that it surprises me, burning just a little as it goes down.

"Now that one *really* tastes like sex," I say.

"I know," you tell me, smiling as I open my eyes.

One breast has come free from the skimpy red bikini top; your nipple pokes out just over the edge.

I drink more water, take the cutting board away from you and set it on the little metal table.

Then I grab your shoulders.

"What are you doing?" you ask.

"Dirtying my palate," I say, and push you onto the chaise longue as I slide out of it.

You're giggling as I reach for your bottoms. You don't even protest that the neighbors might see—any neighbor still watching wants to see whatever he or she can. You struggle a little getting into the chaise longue, but you don't protest. I get my fingers under the string of your bikini bottoms and pull them down quickly.

Your face is flushed with the sun and with the taste of sex. You tuck your breasts back into the bikini top.

"Oh, no you don't," I say, and I reach up and pull the top down.

My hands caress your ripe tomatoes as my mouth descends between your parted thighs. The memory of the tomato's musk complements your taste, and it fills my mouth as I reach out with one hand and seize a warm tomato slice, popping it into your mouth.

You moan faintly around the crushed pulp of the tomato. Red juice runs down your chin.

My tongue slides between your lips and I taste that you're wet—so wet juice runs down my chin, too. I put another tomato slice in your mouth as my tongue finds your clit, and your tomato-muffled moan rises in volume.

Then you're quiet, laying back in the chaise longue and panting softly as I caress your clit with my tongue.

When I slip another tomato slice into your mouth, you seize my fingers and suckle them, coating them with tomato juice. It runs down my wrist and dribbles onto your round, bare breasts. I press my tongue harder against your clit and your back arches.

Tomato juice dribbles down your neck and joins the juice already coating your breasts, soaking the bikini. Lucky it's red. Your moans rise in volume and pitch, and you're very close to coming.

I've got you right on the edge when I lift my face from your pussy, pull down my shorts, and climb onto the chaise longue with you.

Your eyes are closed in rapture, your mouth hanging halfway open, your lips slicked with juice. I put another slice on your tongue, and you suckle it hungrily as my lips press to yours, my tongue delving in to the taste of tomato and of you. My cock finds your lips and eases neatly between them. You're so wet I don't have to wait.

You come almost as soon as I enter you, moaning into my mouth, your breath then coming fast and short as I suck the tomato pulp out of your mouth and savor it hungrily. I fuck you fast, my hands on your breasts, squeezing gently. You're still thrashing and whimpering in orgasm when I come, letting out a thunderous moan and plunging deep inside you as my cock explodes. I slump onto you, licking the juice from the underside of your throat.

"Don't you love tomato season?" you ask.

"I love every season," I tell you. "Just wait until the squash is ready."

Arizona, Ireland, New England
By Cheyenne Blue

Every year, summer comes to the Arizona desert, although some say it never leaves. And summer comes to Ireland, although some say it never really arrives.

Jessamy emails Dara, a woman she's never met, although she knows her better than she knows her own sister. They met in an Internet chat room, although both of them have forgotten which one. It's unimportant now. What matters is their friendship, and they exchange copious emails every day. They talk about important things: how to stretch their unemployment benefits, their neighbors, their infrequent middle-aged nights out, and whether Irish boxty is more like American grits or potato pancakes.

Dara tells Jessamy about the greenness and the quaintness of Ireland, painting a picture of a tranquil, rural life, where donkeys carry the turf to white-painted cottages, a story as appealing as it is inventive. And in return, Jessamy relates tales of coyotes, saguaro cacti reaching imploring arms to brilliant skies, and the merciless Arizona sun that shrivels all to bleached bones, a tale as fascinating as it is tall.

Dara sits in her tumbledown stone cottage in County Cork, which reeks of damp, and says wistfully, wouldn't it be a grand thing indeed if she could see the desert blooms for herself. She dreams of wide, white landscapes, and rattlesnakes in the laundry, and wakes in the morning with the smell of sage in her nostrils.

Jessamy slouches in her trailer on the edge of Tucson, wishing the landlord would repair the air conditioning, and agrees. Dara would love the desert, and she, Jessamy, would love the curling turf and emerald wash of Ireland. She imagines a checked apron and herself carefully putting hens' eggs into the pockets.

A plan is made. They will swap houses for the summer, meeting when their flights connect in Boston, to hand over the keys, and again on the return trip to exchange tales.

They know each other instantly. The fuzzy scanned photos don't do justice, of course, but they link arms like the bosom pals they are, and share a cab to the Holiday Inn. Two nights they have; two nights to see if their friendship translates into Real Life.

The friendship does more than merely translate, and on the first night one offers, the other accepts, and the air-conditioned room on the seventh floor turns into a trysting house. They explore, pressing and caressing flesh that is so familiar, yet eerily strange. Jessamy hovers, then delves between Dara's spread thighs, and bites and laps, curling female moisture onto her tongue. Dara tastes of clover honey, she thinks fancifully, and dreams of lapping the cream from the top of a pint of Guinness.

Dara fingers and fondles, pistoning assertively into golden-pink yielding flesh, and curls her fingers around to seek the pleasure points. She compares the rush of moisture to the summer monsoons, which turn the arroyos into rushing torrents. She suckles at her lover's breast, and traces the suntan lines with her tongue. At the end of the summer she will be like this—a tawny creature, with long limbs of sun-gilded skin, and heat-streaked hair.

Jessamy compares her dark, dry hide to Dara's softer skin, clotted cream pale. The gentle Irish summer will curl Jessamy's hair, soften it so that it hangs in springy curls on her shoulders. The temperate climate will be kind to her body, and she thinks of lazy days in a tiny bathroom with floral curtains at the windows, stroking lotion scented like tea roses into her skin. She runs gentle hands over her lover's flesh, feeling the slight catch as her rougher hands slide over skin as smooth as water.

Dara undulates up her lover's body to catch her lips in a kiss as fierce as the wind that curls along the desert pavement, whipping the sand into swirling eddies that beat against exposed tender flesh. Her tongue plunges deep, stabbing like cactus spines into flinching flesh. Dara's hands are firm, running in assertive patterns, pinching a nipple, biting on a yielding inner thigh, so that the bruise blooms, cloudy, crushed-purple marks of possession.

Jessamy yields, her body melting bonelessly into the bed, soft, springy like the sodden tea-colored turf, as she raises a leg and clasps Dara so that her head is encompassed between her fleshy thighs. Dara's mouth can now flicker with glorious friction on Jessamy's sex, so that the orgasm builds, slowly, wetly, until it breaks in a sungold-crimson tide, sweeping her away from the Holiday Inn.

In a fluid motion, their positions change, and Jessamy pushes and rubs, a deliberate finger frottage, exploring through folds and damp crevices. She insinuates her way so slowly, stimulating so gently that Dara is not aware of the rising climax until it seeps over her, washing from fingers to toes, swelling outward from her sex in deep, dark pulses.

Their sleep is disturbed by dreams, fractured images of waking dreams to come. Dara dreams of how the light will fall clear and sharp over the Sonoran Desert. How she will fearlessly sweep a scorpion from the kitchen bench with a swift flick of a tea towel. She imagines Mexicans with inscrutable eyes, selling papaya in the market place. Jessamy falls into dreams of drowning; black tea pools of bogland, hazy in the twilight, blurred by the soft rain. Herself, sipping on a pint, playing the fiddle with men in tweed caps, her foot tapping the rhythm.

By day, the women explore Boston. Jessamy buys a porcelain coyote figurine, a bandana around its neck, head raised and howling. She will stand it on Dara's bathroom window ledge, next to the red-haired girl in a step-dancing costume that she knows is there, and it will remind her of what she's left. In an Irish shop, Dara buys a St. Brigid's cross, woven not of reeds but shaped in clay. She will hang it above the doorway of Jessamy's trailer, above the Navajo rug on the floor, and it will be a small image of home in an alien landscape.

That night, they return to the Holiday Inn and they return to each other, falling onto the bed with indecent haste, shedding clothes, baring flesh to latch onto a nipple, part pale or golden thighs and dive between. The Holiday Inn is insulated from the real world outside; the summer can't penetrate its walls, and the air conditioning negates any trace of heat or humidity. But to Dara, the room and her lover are as exotic as the surreal cacti that she'll see tomorrow. The sharp taste of Jessamy's cunt is as unusual as the *nopales* and scrambled eggs she'll eat for her first Arizona breakfast. Taking the razor she uses to shave her underarms, she scrapes her lover's pussy bare so that the folds stand out in stark relief. A paradox; bare abraded flesh outside, but inside, secret moist places, slick as summer rain.

Jessamy considers the razor but sets it aside. She tangles her fingers in Dara's abundant thatch of turf-dark pubic hair, parting sodden curls to find the drowned, wet depths they guard. To her, this room is secret and dark, and the things they do here will be forever held close to her heart. As mysterious and strange as the holy shrine where she'll light a candle tomorrow.

That night, neither of them dreams.

###

Every morning, Dara opens the door of Jessamy's trailer, sketches the sign of the cross, gives a quick flicker of acknowledgement to the St. Brigid's cross above the door, and sits down on the step with a cup of tea. She stares at the desert and shudders as a centipede runs across her foot. Then she goes into the small kitchen to cook what passes for bacon here, throwing the scraps into open bins, which will be raided by scavenging coyotes. Later in bed, Dara will shiver under the thin sheet as she listens to their snarls and prays that they don't attack her.

Jessamy shivers, stepping into the damp bathroom. Every day, the mold creeps further across the ceiling, an advancing olive bloom. She bemoans the absence of real coffee, and sits inside at the kitchen table, watching the rain stream down the small panes. Turning the heating up another notch, she contemplates a visit to the village shop, where, once again, she will not understand a word of the thick local accents. Later, she will go to the pub and stare into a pint of Guinness, trying to convince herself she likes the taste.

Both women dream of two nights to come in New England.

Baby, It's Hot Outside
By Delilah Night

It's a Christmas miracle! Please, God, let me have the time to give Mr. Gorgeous my number before Erik the Twerp clears customs. Why did his flight have to land early?

The man attached to the ass I'd been ogling spoke. "Caroline? Is that you?"

"Erik?" I hadn't recognized him. No Xbox controller. No backwards baseball cap. No failed attempt at a moustache. "Wow! You look great!"

I'm going to hell. Thou shalt not lust after thy little brother's friends, even if they're 29. Stop thinking about his butt and focus on walking him to the car without jumping him.

"I really appreciate the offer to take me in for the holiday. I expected to be back in New York by now, but like Jake told you, negotiations—" Erik stopped. "Holy shit, Carrie, it's a billion degrees here."

"Welcome to the tropics." Exiting a building is akin to receiving a hot, wet slap across the face 365 days a year.

For a moment, I thought Erik might dive back into the air-conditioned comfort of the airport.

Taking his suitcase, I rolled my eyes. "Don't worry, Frosty, I won't let you melt."

Several days passed, during which I played tour guide. In daylight hours, I wore the familiar sensible shoes of Jake's pedantic big sister. Exploring Little India inspired a lecture on the multi-ethnic culture of Singapore. I bullied Erik into posing for a photo by the Merlion fountain while holding forth on how it became a symbol of the city.

As daylight shifted into night, though, things changed. My undernourished sex drive was surely why I'd thought Erik was flirting with me at dinner. Accepting a bite of food from his fork didn't mean anything.

The sight of Erik asleep on my couch had me reaching for the aircon remote. Had he always had those abs under his stupid Nirvana t-shirts? A love trail disappeared into frayed cotton pajama bottoms. The urge to step into stripper heels and mount him was almost overwhelming.

There is a Singlish word—cannot—which means "'No, not in a million years. Don't even think about it.'"

My little brother's best friend stirring my libido? Cannot, Caroline. Cannot.

As we joined the thronging Christmas Eve crowds along the retail mecca of Orchard Road, Erik took my hand. The electric shock that flew from my fingers to my clit could've powered the Christmas lights displays that stretched as far as the eye could see. Had to be my imagination that his thumb was caressing my palm.

Cannot.

We stopped to people watch and enjoy ice cream. It wasn't the dessert I pictured as my tongue lapped at the dripping cream.

Licking. Stroking. Suck—

"Is that band playing 'Let it Snow'?" Erik interrupted my train of thought.

"Yes."

"Wouldn't snow on the equator be a sign of a nuclear winter?"

I snickered. "One of the malls does a nightly show where the Christmas tree shoots soapy foam out of the top, and they call it a snow storm. It's a big—but, likely chemical-laden—hit with the kiddos."

Maybe you'd like to discuss dengue fever as an encore, Carrie? No wonder you haven't been laid in forever. Cannot.

"It's pretty awesome that you have this whole life here." He casually draped an arm about my shoulders. "Are you still close with people from home?"

Resting my head against his shoulder, *like friends do*, I shrugged. "A few. Josh."

"I never liked Josh," Erik remarked.

"Why?" My high school boyfriend had always been a sweetie.

"Why do you think? I was crazy about you. You only noticed I was alive when you kicked Jake and me out of the living room."

101

"That's not true. I noticed you were alive whenever you ate the last slice of pizza, too." Sarcasm was my crumbling wall of defense against desire.

Down, girl. CANNOT.

"Three days with you, and I feel like a lovesick idiot all over again." Erik gave a bitter laugh. "I sound like a fucking idiot, too."

Our eyes locked. As one, we turned and began the walk back toward my apartment.

Fingers traced the thin line of skin between the top of my shorts and the bottom of my tank top as we walked. Erik's arms wrapped around me, pulling me against his chest at each red light. Arousal grew with each passing intersection. Did the colorful illumination from the Christmas lights highlight or hide that my nipples were erect?

One more second was too long to wait. I grabbed Erik's hand and pulled him into the Botanical Gardens. We were still five minutes from my apartment. Silently, I led him away from the well-lit path. Once hidden in shadows, we stopped. The moisture between my thighs couldn't be blamed on humidity.

It was one thing to burn my way through every battery in my house trying to cool my libido. It was entirely another to deliberately jump into the fire.

Anyone who chooses to live in a land of eternal summer shouldn't be scared of heat.

"Caroline," he murmured.

I twined my arms around his neck and pressed my lips to Erik's.

Can. CAN.

When I was little, I used to have a collection of snow globes. I'd shake them until the blizzard inside obliterated the miniature scenes. The touch of Erik's lips on mine created the same effect; everything but him was erased from existence.

A hand slid under my top and took possession of a breast. Fingers rolled a hard, sensitive nipple as our tongues danced.

Although free to grab the ass that had first caught my eye, I was more tempted by other anatomy. I fell to my knees in front of Erik. The button fly was open in seconds. My hands explored the length I couldn't quite see. I learned the path of the vein on the underside of his shaft.

Will it be sweet and gentle? Or the kind of pounding that leaves a delicious soreness for days?

I dedicated myself to fulfilling every dirty image that had flicked through my mind as we'd eaten ice cream. Hot flesh, rather than frozen dessert was licked with enthusiasm. Saltiness, rather than sweet, dripped onto my tongue. The head of his cock was granted entry to my mouth with tantalizing slowness.

"Carrie, you're killing me!"

I pulled him deep into my mouth and set a demanding pace.

Erik's hands fisted in my hair as he chanted, "...spread you open. Fuck you so hard. Spank that sweet ass of yours."

Having soaked through my panties, arousal drooled down my thighs.

On your knees in return, licking me until I've come so many times I can't stand.

"Caroline!" Erik's cock strained, then spasmed, as his orgasm filled my mouth.

We broke apart, breathing heavily. The roar of an engine on a nearby road shattered the quiet.

"You know, I think it's too hot for us to finish your tour of Singapore. I'd hate to confess to people back home that I let you get heatstroke," I said with mock innocence.

I could feel Erik's smirk forming, even in the dark. He hauled me to my feet and kissed me thoroughly. "We can't have that. I guess we'll just have to take refuge in your air conditioning."

CAN!

Summer School
By Rachel Kramer Bussel

I never liked school as a kid, though I kept trying to find ways to make it interesting. I loved to read, and even got in trouble for reading books under the table. Even college, where we could take weird electives involving everything from space exploration to *Game of Thrones*, wasn't for me. So once I left, I didn't think the word "school" would apply to my life ever again.

Then I started selling sex toys. At first, it was just a side gig, a way to make some extra money. My real job was selling makeup, so I figured they could go hand in hand. I decided to invite some of the women who were my best customers—not just the ones who spent the most, but the ones who fed me juicy gossip while I painted their faces—over for cocktails and cock rings. It was June, the weather just turning from a lackluster spring to a sunny, sparkling summer.

The first time, there was a lot of giggling. But once that was over, the six women were racing to order all sorts of vibrators. I made more that night than I made in a week of slinging lipstick and mascara. I thought I had it made in the shade; I told Todd that our summer was off to a very good start.

Then the phone calls and emails started. "So...what do I do with these handcuffs, exactly?" "I'm not sure how to use this butt plug." "Kyle wants me to talk dirty but I don't know what to say." Every last one of them had questions. So I decided our next meeting would be a class of sorts. Summer Sex School, I called it in an email.

Elaine wrote back first. "Can I bring Nate? I just don't think I'll be able to remember everything. Plus he's...curious." The way she said "curious" made it sound like Nate thought I was hosting an orgy or something. I said I'd think about it. I was all set to say no, because what do I know about being a teacher, let alone sex? Not that Todd and I don't have fun in bed, but we're not going crazy with whips and chains or anything.

But when every last one of them asked if she could bring her guy, I had to agree, if some of them were okay sitting on the floor. I made Todd quiz me over and over about all the products. "Honey, you're taking this too seriously. It should be fun. It's not like they're being graded. It's sex. And toys. I can stay if you want some moral support."

"Okay."

"And maybe instead of giving speeches I should use some of these on you so you can speak from experience."

"Like what?" I asked, suspicious.

"Whatever you want."

"You want to?"

"Don't say it like that. Of course, I want to. Why not?" He paused. "You're giving me that look that means you're mad. Baby, everyone uses sex toys. Okay, not everyone, but a lot of people. Didn't it give you those statistics in the brochure? Not that it matters what everyone else is doing. I'm just saying that...they look fun. You could use them on me." His face turned soft and hopeful. I inched closer to him.

"Do you want me to use them on you?" Maybe I wouldn't feel so threatened if I did. *You shouldn't feel threatened at all*, I told myself, but that didn't stop the feeling from creeping up.

"Strip and lie down," I ordered in a gruffer voice than I'd ever used with him. Todd did as instructed. He's so tall he takes up the length of the bed. I eyed the selection of sample toys in their jumble of pink, purple, red, blue, black and white. I selected a small pink vibrator, straddled him, and turned it on. Todd's eyes closed as he sank back against the pillow while I lightly touched the buzzing toy to his nipple. A corresponding ripple made his body dance beneath me. I tried the other nipple, then went back to the first while taking the neglected one into my mouth. Todd let out a strangled sound. As soon as I'd let my teeth nip his nub, I stopped, turning off the toy as well.

His eyes shot open, begging me to continue. "Please." That one word said it all; I felt it straight between my legs. I turned around, raising my ass so he could get a good glimpse. The toy had pointy ears but a round base. I turned it on and let the round part brush against his balls.

In this position, I could see his cock getting harder right before my eyes, the tip glistening just for me. I teased his inner thighs with the vibrator as I licked the salty treat from him. He reached for my ass, and for a second I was tempted to stop and whip out one of the many types of handcuffs I now possessed, but it felt too good.

Todd prised my cheeks open as I let the toy and my mouth work in tandem. He moaned, the sound at once familiar and foreign, deeper and needier than his usual sex noises. As I leaned forward to take more of him in my mouth, I shut off my buzzing buddy. I'm only so good at multitasking. Todd didn't object—in fact, he pulled me close and planted his mouth right where I wanted it. He filled me with his cock and his tongue at once, our bodies joined, and certainly still buzzing. As he worked me over, I teased him with the tip of my tongue. Todd's thumb slid to my clit as he licked me quickly, with strokes he knows are guaranteed to make me come. I shook against him, a whole body high. I slowed down as my orgasm took over, keeping only the tip in my mouth. Once my tremors had subsided, I sucked him until I was rewarded with his cream.

When I shifted to curl up next to him, Todd said, "So, Teach, ready for class?"

###

We kept on practicing right up until the decisive evening. It's a good thing, too, because when someone whispered, "Can you show us how to put on these nipple clamps?" I didn't hesitate. They say those who can, do, and those who can't, teach, but that's not entirely true. I can do both, and during that class I showed off a butt plug, a vibrator, clamps, a gag and a tickler. I sold out my stock, and scheduled a whole summer's worth of classes. Turns out I don't actually hate school; I just needed to find the right one for me.

Night Swimming
By Justine Elyot

Everyone else is in bed.

You have slipped out of bed and into a floaty silk robe, leaving him asleep, exhausted by the exertions of the night before. You step out on to the balcony and note that the sky has that foreign, endless darkness so rarely seen in the city; only a sliver of moon interrupts it. The warmth of the day lingers in the air, accentuating the heavy scents of jasmine and honeysuckle. You stretch your limbs as you walk across the cool tiles, shaking out the weariness and muscle ache, but there is no escape from the telltale twinges. What would soothe where healing balms have failed?

Your eye travels downward to the moonlit pool. The faint lapping sound of the water entices you down the steps, lures you across the terrace until you are standing at the edge, looking down at the midnight ripples. Yes, this is what will ease your burning muscles.

You shrug off the gown and dip a toe in the shallows. It is not as warm as it would be by day, but the remains of the sun's ferocity have kept the edge of cold away. You walk slowly down the gentle slope, feeling the water tickle and caress your feet, then your ankles, then your calves, then your thighs and then it is all over and around your naked body to chest height, comfortably lukewarm.

You swish and swirl around for a minute or two, making waves and splashes, then you tilt backwards and float, relishing your weightlessness and the unusual opportunity to stare upwards without having to squint against the sun. You could not see them before, but now tiny silver puncture marks in the black silk sky glint and twinkle down at you. You drift around the pool like this, closing your eyes and letting the pleasant, heated memories of the last few days play against your eyelids until they start to merge and mutate and make no sense...you are almost asleep...

Something is making waves, threatening to capsize the vessel of your body, and you come to with a start, flapping with agitation and looking for the bottom of the pool with your feet. From behind, an arm grabs you about the waist, and a hand claps down on your mouth before you can squawk protest.

"Out for a little swim in the moonlight, are we?" murmurs a familiar voice into your ear, and your squirms lose their urgency, your screams turn to sighs. He removes his hand from your mouth and you turn your head so that your lips can meet his, kissing hungrily while he runs expert fingers over your slippery body, finally cupping your breasts and half-turning you around in the water, lifting your feet so that you are weightless. Now he and the water conspire to manipulate your body to his behest; he hoists you up so that you straddle his hips and he cradles your back loosely, encouraging you to bend over backwards so that your hair fans out like anemone fronds on the surface of the pool. He leans down over you and his tongue traces a path from the hollow of your throat, lapping at the dewy drops of water beaded on your skin, under the curve of your breasts, over the gentle bumps of your ribcage, lusciously licking around your navel while your legs thrash up wavy crests, disturbing the placidity of the surface.

"Enough of that," his voice vibrates over your stomach before he rises up to his full height again, flipping you over so quickly that you almost swallow a mouthful of your aqueous surroundings. His hands hold firm on your haunches, thumbs spreading the insides of your thighs while your arms flounder, working to keep your head above water. Tiny wavelets of tepidity tickle at your open sex, then they are joined by a warm, flexible pressure and you half cry out, shuddering in delightful recognition of his tongue. It mixes with the water, lapping and drinking your diluted essence while his hands continue to hold you and open you further. You drown in the sensation, and almost drown for real when the intensity temporarily makes you forget to keep your face out of the water. Your hands splash at the water and your gargle out a blissful orgasm, undulating like a mermaid caught in the overwhelming current of his undivertable intent.

"Hmmm, wet...and willing..." he intones, then he amuses himself by pulling and pushing you through the water like an aquatic tango dancer, swirling and whooshing you through the darkened cool until the pool is choppy and foamy and you are breathless, giggling with exhilaration.

Now he has you pressed up against the side of the pool, out of your depth but not his; your arms cling around his neck and your back is suctioned to the mosaic tiles. He swarms between your legs, adjusts you so that you have no escape from his steely submarine tumescence and proceeds to spear you, thrusting upwards, languidly at first until it is clear that you are secure and buoyant enough to take any pace or angle he prefers. The cool moisture that softens your skin is heating up, evaporating, turning to beads of perspiration, sticking and clinging to his chest, gluing you together so that you are like one writhing merperson, joined at the lips and below. Tidal waves gush around you, showers of froth rain upon you, you kick up fountains of passion, drenching him and you until there is wailing and grunting and howling and moaning and sighing and silence.

And applause.

You squint over his shoulder in a daze, seeing that the balcony lights are on and your fellow vacationers are dotted about the terrace, some clapping, others snogging.

"Well, we're happy to entertain you," you pout to them. "Who's next?"

There is general shedding of robes and a barefoot stampede across the tiles.

You and your lover laugh as the stilled pool explodes into life around you.

When in Nice
By Alison Tyler

In Nice, the ladies go around topless at the beach. This is something I've known for years, since I first overheard a coworker discussing her trip to France back when I was a college intern. No tops. I don't know why the image stuck, but I could imagine myself walking on a white sand beach, pale lemon bikini bottoms on, tie top covering my small breasts. A blanket spread. And then me, pulling a string to reveal myself, sitting up and staring at the waves while the sun lapped at my body.

There was something, some fantasy woven in. How free I would feel to sit on my blanket and let the world see me. But when I finally got to Nice, when after years of scrimping, after losing a job and a boyfriend in the same month, finding myself for once momentarily free, I couldn't pull the string.

I wasn't twenty-two anymore. That's what I told myself as I sat on the blanket, wearing that lemon-yellow bikini but with a cover up on top. I wasn't thirty-two either. My long dark hair still reached the middle of my back, but there were streaks of silver in the front. Other women were topless. They were all ages, all shapes. And they were what I wanted to be.

Free.

I sat there on my blanket and I watched the waves and

I thought, *I'm in Nice. When in Nice...*but that's as far as got. Usually, I was in Cleveland. And when in Cleveland you don't take your top off—and there isn't any beach. Well, there's Lake Erie, of course, or an eight-hour drive to Atlantic City. But when you're at Lake Erie, you don't take off your top.

On the third day of my vacation—or really, my escape, because that's what this felt like, an escape to France—I noticed a man on a nearby towel. He smiled at me, and I smiled back, and that was all the encouragement he needed. He came over, and I prepared myself with my little handbook of French phrases. "I don't speak French." That was bookmarked. "I don't even speak a little bit of French." I'd cobbled that one together. "I'm from Cleveland." In case it wasn't obvious from the tote bag at my side proudly proclaiming "I heart Ohio."

"Beautiful weather," he said in perfect English, and I smiled, relieved and nodded. "Do you speak English?" he asked next, and I thought, *Oh my. He thinks I could be French.* For a split second, I considered pretending to not speak English. Because I was so flattered that he thought I didn't. But I couldn't cast myself in some misguided sitcom plot. Laverne or Shirley I'm not. So I said, "Yes, I am, and it is, and I'm Toni." I'd never been Toni before. I'd always been Antonia. So I wouldn't be French. At least, I'd be someone new.

He laughed. "That's my line."

"What do you mean?"

He sat on the edge of my blanket. "*I'm* Tony."

It felt like the opening of a chick flick, and I needed a chick flick. I needed one real bad. But in a movie, I'd have possessed a script. In reality, I said, "Isn't that something?" and wanted to kick myself in the head.

"I don't usually talk to women I don't know," he said. "But I figured...when in Nice."

"Do people in Nice talk to strangers?" I asked.

"I mean," he said, and he looked as unsure of himself as I felt, "that this is a new place a new experience for me, and I kind of wanted to grab onto it with both hands."

That's exactly how I felt, and I told him, and then in a rush I told him the rest. How I wanted to go topless, but I couldn't seem to find the will to pull the string.

"I'll pull your string," he said, and then he blushed. He blushed. That was my job.

I couldn't help myself. I started laughing, and he blushed even more. "I'm sorry," I told him. "I've been living in a stifling relationship for far too long. I thought going to Europe would be freeing, but I probably should have taken baby steps. I ought to have gone overnight somewhere close by, a motel with a concrete hole in the ground for a pool. Rather than jump headfirst into the Mediterranean."

He moved closer to me, and then he held my hand. "We could go slow together," he said. "And I could untie your string, but I could do it tonight. When nobody's around."

Topless in the moonlight? That sounded a bit like a fruity drink with a pink umbrella.

"Meet me here," he said. "At sundown."

I thought about it. I thought what that would mean. The waiting. The talking myself up and talking myself down. I looked at him and said, "Fuck going slow."

He seemed surprised, but he didn't move. I turned my back, and then peeked over my shoulder. "Pull my string," I said. "Pull it."

He looked as shocked to hear me say the words as I was to hear myself say them. He pulled the string. I felt the flutter of the bikini fall down. I felt my heart flutter in the same way. I faced him as I took the top all the way off.

And then I did something even more shocking: I kissed him. He didn't pull back or push me away. He kissed me in return, and I felt the sun's heat from the outside, and a new kind of heat on the inside, and I saw the rest of the day unfolding like a brilliant blue towel on a white-sand beach.

We would go back to my hotel. We would get naked there. We would do things I'd never had the nerve to do before.

In Cleveland, this would never have happened.

But when in Nice....

About the Authors

Primula Bond is an Oxford-educated cougar masquerading as a respectable wife and mother with three sons. She has been writing erotic short stories and novels for Black Lace and Xcite Books for more than 20 years, but in the last year has hit the bestseller lists with her latest erotic *Unbreakable Trilogy*, published by Avon Books for Harper Collins. The three books, *The Silver Chain*, *The Golden Locket* and *The Diamond Ring*, chart the passionate love story of Gustav Levi and Serena Folkes where sexual attraction mixes with jealousy, betrayal and danger. Primula has also given readings and workshops at various writing festivals in the UK and also works as a book doctor for the online critique service for aspiring writers, Writers Workshop. Join in the gossip and chat with Primula on Twitter @primulabond , befriend her on Facebook, and check out her blog www.primulabond.blogspot.com

At an early age, **Angell Brooks** decided to put the voices in her head to good use. These days, they're a little sexier, a whole lot kinkier, but they still like to play in the sand box. Find her characters in books by Cleis, December Ink, and Harlequin Spice.

Author and editor **Tenille Brown** is featured in *Going Down, Best Bondage Erotica 2011* and *2012, Suite Encounters, Best Lesbian Erotica 2013, Only You, Sudden Sex, Baby Got Back* and *The Big Book of Orgasms*. Her first anthology, *Can't Get Enough*, is published by Cleis Press. Tenille blogs at www.therealtenille.com.

Rachel Kramer Bussel (rachelkramerbussel.com) is the editor of *The Big Book of Orgasms; Gotta Have It: 69 Stories of Sudden Sex; Baby Got Back: Anal Erotica; Women in Lust; Cheeky Spanking Stories; Please, Sir; Please, Ma'am; The Mile High Club; Suite Encounters: Hotel Sex Stories* and many other sexy anthologies.

Over the past 12 years, **Cheyenne Blue**'s erotica has appeared in more than 90 anthologies including *Best Women's Erotica, Cowboy Lust, Best Lesbian Romance, Best Lesbian Erotica,* and *Morning, Noon and Night*. She lives and writes by the beach in the endless summer of Queensland, Australia. Visit her website at www.cheyenneblue.com

Kathleen Delaney-Adams is a stone high femme porn author and spoken word performer. The artistic director of BODY HEAT: Femme Porn Tour, Kathleen's erotic fiction will be featured in several kinky, smutty anthologies set for release in 2014 and 2015, including *She Who Must Be Obeyed* and *The Big Book of Submission: 69 Kinky Tales*.

May Deva writes from her East Coast home, surrounded by more strays than she should mention in polite company. An avid voyeur of life, she draws most of her inspiration from secrets and closed doors, or what she imagines might happen behind them. You can check her out on Twitter as @maydeva.

Justine Elyot has written loads of books and short stories since appearing on the scene with *On Demand* (Black Lace) in 2009. Her latest novel is *Master of the House* (Mischief 2014). More details are available on her website www.justineelyot.com or from the horse's mouth at Twitter (twitter.com/justineelyot) and Facebook (www.facebook.com/justine.elyot).

Emerald's (www.TheGreenLightDistrict.org) erotic fiction has been included in anthologies published by Cleis Press, Mischief, and Logical-Lust. She serves an assistant newsletter editor and Facebook group moderator for Marketing for Romance Writers (MFRW) and is an advocate for reproductive choice, sex worker rights, and sexual freedom.

Lucy Felthouse is a very busy woman! She writes erotica and erotic romance in a variety of subgenres and pairings, and has more than 100 publications to her name, with many more in the pipeline. These include several editions of *Best Bondage Erotica*, *Best Women's Erotica 2013* and *Best Erotic Romance 2014*. Another string to her bow is editing, and she has edited and co-edited a number of anthologies, and also edits for a small publishing house. She owns Erotica For All, is book editor for Cliterati, and is one eighth of The Brit Babes. Find out more at www.lucyfelthouse.co.uk. Join her on www.facebook.com/lucyfelthousewriter as well as www.twitter.com/cw1985, and subscribe to her newsletter at: eepurl.com/gMQb9

Tamsin Flowers loves to write light-hearted erotica, often with a twist in the tail/tale and a sense of fun. In the words of one reviewer, "Ms Flowers has a way of describing sexual tension that forces itself upon your own body." Her stories have appeared in a wide variety of anthologies, for publishers including Cleis Press, Xcite Books, House of Erotica and Go Deeper Press. She has now graduated to novellas and novels—for Xcite Books, Secret Cravings Publishing and Totally Bound—with the intention of penning her magnum opus in the very near future. In the meantime, like most erotica writers, she finds herself working on at least ten stories at once: while she figures out whose leg belongs in which story, you can find out more about her at www.tamsinflowers.com or tamsinflowers.blogspot.co.uk/

Jodie Griffin loves chocolate and alliterative titles, sees the dirty side in pretty much everything, and needs more hours in every day. She writes naughty tales about nice girls and the men who love them. Visit Jodie at www.jodiegriffin.com.

A.M. Hartnett began writing erotica upon receiving what, at the time, she considered very bad advice from a career counselor. Her stories have appeared on the web, in ebooks, and in various anthologies, including Kristina Wright's *Best Erotic Romance* series and Rachel Kramer Bussel's *Curvy Girls*. She lives in Atlantic Canada and can be reached by visiting www.amhartnett.com.

Elise Hepner writes smutty goodness for Entangled, Ellora's Cave, Xcite, and Secret Cravings Publishing. She frequently contributes to Cleis Press anthologies including *Never Say Never* and *Best Bondage Erotica 2012*. She lives with her husband and two clingy kitties in Maryland. Visit www.elisehepner.com to learn more and explore her backlist.

Delilah Night is an American expat living in Singapore. You can find Delilah's work in *Nine-to-Five Fantasies* edited by Alison Tyler, *Irresistible* edited by Rachel Kramer Bussel, and *Glitter* edited by Mona Darling. Her website is www.delilahnight.com

Teresa Noelle Roberts (www.teresanoelleroberts.com) writes sexy stories for lusty romantics of all persuasions. Her short fiction appears in *The Mammoth Book of Erotic Romance and Domination; Best Erotic Romance 2013; Best Bondage Erotica 2011, 2012, 2013* and *2014; Mammoth Book of Best New Erotica 12;* and other provocatively titled anthologies. She has also published numerous kinky and/or paranormal romance novels. She swears this story wasn't inspired by real life, but since she makes up stories for a living, it's hard to know when she's telling the truth.

Thomas S. Roche is the author of the zombie thriller *The Panama Laugh* and the short story collections *Dark Matter* and *Matching Skirt and Kneepads*. He has written several hundred published short stories in the horror, fantasy and erotica genres. He has also been a volunteer training instructor at San Francisco Sex Information (www.sfsi.org) for more than a decade. He can be found on the web at www.thomasroche.com, www.twitter.com/thomasroche, as well as www.facebook.com/skidroche.

Willsin Rowe (willsinrowe.blogspot.com) falls in love with a scent, a playful expression or an act of casual intimacy more easily than with physical beauty. When confronted by any combination of these he is a lost cause. He has done many things over and over. He has done even more things only once. He has half-done more things than he cares to admit. He is intelligent but not sensible. He is polite but inappropriate. He is passionate but fearful. He is honest but reticent. He is not scruffy enough nor stylish enough to be cool.

Donna George Storey (www.DonnaGeorgeStorey.com) is the author of *Amorous Woman*, an erotic novel based on her own experiences living in Japan. Her adults-only tales appeared in numerous places including *Penthouse, The Mammoth Book of Erotica Presents the Best of Donna George Storey, Best Women's Erotica, Never Say Never*, and *The Big Book of Orgasms*. She also writes a regular column on writing, erotica and sexuality for the Erotica Readers and Writers blog.

Sammi Lou Thorne grew up and has spent her life so far in the small towns and wide-open spaces of the Western United States. She found her love of writing at a young age, and while working at an online adult store several years ago, she developed an interest in writing erotica and exploring her personal boundaries through her stories and in real life. Her characters are an extension of her life, her fantasies, and the people she knows, and her stories are often a reflection of her experiences and desires.

Alison Tyler (alisontyler.blogspot.com) has edited fifty collections for Cleis Press, a trio for Harlequin, and a handful for Pretty Things Press. Her most recent novels are *Dark Secret Love* and *The Delicious Torment*. Sommer Marsden helped her through some of her darkest times, and she is ever grateful.

Sophia Valenti (sophiavalenti.blogspot.com) prefers hot summer nights over crisp fall days and fire-engine red lipstick over pretty pink gloss. She lives in New York City in an apartment with too many books and too few bookshelves. Her erotic fiction has appeared in anthologies published by Cleis Press, Harlequin Spice and Pretty Things Press. Follow her on Twitter @sophiavalenti.

Previously Published:

"Hot Tomato" by Thomas S. Roche first appeared in *Juicy Erotica*, edited by Alison Tyler. Pretty Things Press, 2003.

Arizona, Ireland, New England by Cheyenne Blue appeared in E Is For Exotic, edited by Alison Tyler, Cleis Press, 2007.

YOU'VE REACHED

"THE END!"

BUY THIS AND MORE TITLES AT
www.eXcessica.com

eXcessica's YAHOO GROUP
groups.yahoo.com/
group/eXcessica/

Check us out for updates about eXcessica books!

Printed in Great Britain
by Amazon